THE GRASS TREE

Why? That was the question Christopher Kershaw asked on that scorchingly hot Australian summer morning in 1851. Why were the Allard family so determined to ruin his life? Kershaw was now in grave financial difficulties and his marriage was foundering. Perhaps his own pride was partly to blame, but the root cause was the Allards' continuing enmity. Twenty-four hours later, in terrifying circumstances, Kershaw had the perfect chance to avenge himself.

Books by Nara Lake
in the Linford Romance Library:

MAN FROM KANPUR
HOSTAGE OF LOVE

NARA LAKE

THE GRASS TREE

Complete and Unabridged

LINFORD
Leicester

First published in Great Britain

First Linford Edition
published 1998

British Library CIP Data

Lake, Nara
   The grass tree.—Large print ed.—
Linford romance library
1. Love stories
2. Large type books
I. Title
823.9'14 [F]

ISBN 0–7089–5306–9

Published by
F. A. Thorpe (Publishing) Ltd.
Anstey, Leicestershire
Set by Words & Graphics Ltd.
Anstey, Leicestershire
Printed and bound in Great Britain by
T. J. International Ltd., Padstow, Cornwall

This book is printed on acid-free paper

1

Christopher Kershaw awoke about three in the morning that Wednesday. His sleep had been restless, aggravated as much by his worries as by the oppressive heat which had shimmered over the town for many days. After a few minutes, he slid carefully out of the mosquito-netted tester bed, aware that his wife was soundly asleep, despite her complaints the previous evening that she had not enjoyed a proper night's rest since the heatwave had commenced.

For a man of his solid just under six feet, he moved quietly, and clad only in his nightshirt, he opened the front door and stepped out under the veranda. February dawn was still an hour away, and the stars hung huge in the black sky. There was a stirring of sounds across the town, of people and animals alike unable to sink into the deep slumber they craved.

He sat down on one of the chairs which formed the veranda furniture, and leaned back, shutting his tired eyes, hoping that he would be able to doze off out here. The air was cooler than indoors, and after this long dry spell, even the mosquitoes were dying off. There had to be something good to think about, and that was it. The mosquitoes were quite definitely not as bad.

He needed to be fresh to face another day. There had been a note left at the store yesterday afternoon requesting that he present himself at the office of Mr Andrew M'Kirk at eight-thirty a.m. regarding a commission.

Now, what did that mean? What sort of commission would a magistrate like Mr Andrew M'Kirk have for him? He prayed that it would be a paid matter, and not a return favour. He needed money desperately, any money, in any amount, however small. He had met M'Kirk once to talk to, on the day of that disgraceful affair with the Allards. Blast their eyes! Why couldn't they have stayed Sydney-side of the Murray instead of coming down here to Melbourne to continue their hounding?

Who would have thought that their sort, so high and mighty, would have bothered to carry a grudge over a small and insignificant incident which had occurred when he was eleven years old?

He remembered the day very well, a Thursday it had been. His father had recently sold some calves, for cash, so that for a change they had some spending money. In spite of the fine day, it was April, with winter and snow on the mountains just weeks ahead, and one object of this family excursion into Bathurst was to buy young Christopher new boots.

He had not liked the idea, after running barefoot all the summer, like a blackfellow. And he remembered that on the way into town, Pa told Ma to buy some new ribbon for her bonnet, because they had been invited to a wedding, a big event in their quiet, hard-working lives. Both the bride and 'groom were natives — that is, born in New South Wales — which was unusual back in 1833, when most people still came from the British Isles. Currency, they called the young ones born in Australia, or else cornstalks, because they were often taller and thinner than their parents from the Old Dart.

Come to think of it, the Allard boys were natives too, for all the grand airs they gave themselves.

It came back so vividly, every detail of that crisp autumn day long ago, with a slight south-westerly breeze and small fluffy clouds floating above the hills. After we had done our shopping, Kershaw mused on his hot veranda, Ma went off visiting, carrying little Joanna, who was about a year old then, and a fair weight for a slight thing like my mother to hold in her arms.

She was so proud of Jo, and who could blame her for wanting to show off the baby, because Ma had not been lucky with babies. Up on the hill behind their farm, there was a small graveyard with two baby brothers and another sister lying beneath little markers. Christopher's father always kept an eye out for nice-looking pebbles in their creek, and arranged them in borders about the graves.

Sometimes, thought the adult Kershaw, I'd see Ma look up that way, and the tears would start out of her eyes and run down her cheeks. Such lovely eyes they were, too, soft and dark and brown, pansy eyes you'd call them.

So, with young Christopher awkward in his new boots, Jonathon Kershaw soon finished his small amount of business, and together father and son sought about for the means to kill time whilst waiting for Mrs Kershaw.

There was not a great deal doing in Bathurst. It had been planned on a grand scale as befitted the first settlement inland from Sydney across the Blue Mountains, but, in the early thirties, it had not progressed past being a scattered collection of small houses, the only building of any size being the convict barracks. The focal point of the town was a large square, a dustbowl in summer and a swamp in winter, and it was here that Christopher beheld the carriage, with two well-matched horses between the shafts and a coachman holding the reins. He gaped at the strange sight, for out here in the west, utility was everything.

Beyond the carriage, a convict iron-gang was engaged in levelling out part of the square, with the chained workers expertly doing as little as possible with the apparent maximum of effort, this accomplishment being widely known as 'The Government Stroke'. They were taking advantage of the fact that their overseer had been diverted into talking with a tall, slim man, elegantly clad in fashionable riding clothes, whose gloved right hand rested casually on the neck of his first-rate bay horse.

Christopher was not interested in this tableau. He was fascinated by the carriage and its occupants. The lady, obviously, was out to make an impression in Bathurst, although the iron-gang and the few persons going about their business did not constitute much of an audience. Because she was seated, her skirts were an unknown quantity, but her sleeves alone were enough to make the ordinary dungaree-clad yokels gape. Out they jutted from her shoulders, emerging from a finely pleated yoke to balloon magnificently to the wrists before being caught into neat cuffs above pale kid gloves, which were revealed as the lady limply raised a hand to brush away a fly.

Her real glory was in her bonnet, a creation which must have been imported from across the world, London, or even Paris. A wide brim was raised a little on the left side, to give a coquettish effect, and the under surface of the brim so revealed was laden with decoration, having ribbons appliqued into a design of roses to match the unlikely blooms which rioted magnificently on the crown, where they mingled with feathers and more ribbons. The amazing confection was held to the lady's well-curled head by strings decorated with lace, and with the addition of a sort of gauze curtain suspended from the back of the edifice, it was altogether enough to provide Bathurst's dowdy housewives with a subject of conversation for days.

Being a normal small boy, Christopher Kershaw gave the lady's bonnet barely a glance, for his gaze was rivetted by the two children, who were seated one on either side of their mother. The bigger lad was about his own age, the other a little younger, and both had chilly blue eyes, pink and white complexions, and golden hair worn rather long. This effeminacy of appearance was enough to put them beyond the pale, but instead of the dungaree garments which formed the uniform worn by the young natives, they were clad, or that part visible of them was clad, in blue coats made from a smooth, soft material, and fussy white shirts. On their heads was what really took them right out of the world of ordinary, grubby, anti-feminine, uncouth, colonial boyhood. Christopher could hardly believe his eyes. In his opinion, any boy with a single drop of red blood in his veins would have lost or destroyed those monstrosities at the first opportunity.

The two boys wore identical blue caps with silk tassels dropping to their shoulders. The local boy, his own battered old cabbage-tree, handed down from his father, on the back of his head, and the brand new boots hurting on his stockingless feet, thrust his hands into his trouser pockets and stared with all the insolence he could muster. If his father had not been there, he would have poked out his tongue. Had he met those unfortunates face to face in some place away from adult supervision, he would not have hesitated to avenge the insult to boys everywhere by flinging mud at their heads.

His father grasped his arm and pulled him forward.

'Come on,' he rasped, in an unusually terse tone of voice. 'That cove on the horse is Captain Allard, him I was assigned to, and your mother too.'

The boy understood immediately. Being assigned, that is, let out as free labour after being transported from Britain, was the system. Once it was over, and a man had done his time and had his freedom, that sort of thing was best forgotten. Out here, as far as the law was concerned, Pa was as good as anyone, and no one could blame him for not wishing to go over and touch his forelock to his former master.

'He's comin' this way,' growled Jonathon Kershaw. 'I'm goin' into the public-house to have a dram. You go and join your mother over at Mrs Haworth's.'

Christopher saw that Captain Allard

had mounted his horse and had turned the animal in their direction.

'All right, Pa,' he responded immediately. His father was not a drinking man, but this was an emergency.

'I'll fetch you when they've gone,' added his father over his shoulder as he disappeared into the ill-lit interior of the glorified shanty which called itself a public-house.

Dismissed, Christopher did not hurry. He knew that it would take at least ten minutes for his father to have that dram, and he dearly wished to have another look at those caps. He was in luck. As he dawdled across the muddy expanse towards Mrs Haworth's neat cottage, set amidst rows of vegetables with the family cow grazing on the vacant land alongside, he saw the carriage wheel about in his direction. As it passed, Captain Allard to the rear, and wheels churning through the mud, the two other boys looked at him, and he poked out his tongue at them, compounding the insult by thrusting both thumbs into his ears and waggling his fingers. The result was gratifying. Two aloof young faces flushed pink with fury, and cold eyes flashed chips of ice. Christopher thrust his hands back into pockets, laughing, and his bare feet no longer felt so cramped and mistreated in the new boots.

Later, his triumph was to be replaced by fear and doubt. Travelling homewards slowly and uncomfortably in the dray, drawn by their old workhorse, Brownie, Jonathon Kershaw seemed even graver and more silent than usual. Likewise, his wife, who in spite of a hard life was usually much given to inconsequential chatter, was quiet and thoughtful. It was some time before she spoke at all, and when she did, Christopher, jammed amidst the stores, felt a weighty guilt settling on him.

'Why do you reckon Captain Allard's here?' she asked, in a funny little voice. 'Do you reckon he saw you?'

Ma sounded frightened, Ma who had

not shown a twinge of fear when she and Pa had been bullied by bushrangers in their own home the previous year.

'At Pete's, they say he's staying with Mr Watts and looking for some land for his sons.'

'But they're only children.'

'I 'spect he reckons he must grab what he can now.'

They said no more at that time, but during the night, as he lay in his bed in the tiny lean-to room at the back of the shack, Christopher heard the soft rise and fall of their voices, and the word 'Allard'. What had he done? Would Captain Allard ride up to the farm in the morning with soldiers behind him, and take Ma and Pa away to serve fresh sentences? How could he look after the farm and little Joanna by himself? Or would Captain Allard content himself with arresting young Christopher?

For days, Christopher started out of his skin every time he fancied he heard approaching hoofbeats. When someone did come on a horse, it turned out to be Mr Watts, who had one of the largest properties in the district. Mr Watts was also a magistrate, and when Christopher saw him, his first impulse was to bolt off into the bush. Mr Watts, however, had not called to serve an order for the family's mass arrest. He wished to enquire whether Mr Kershaw might have a good piece of cheese put away.

'I hope it pleases your guests,' said Kershaw when the small transaction was completed.

'Guests? Oh, they've returned to Captain Allard's place at Liverpool. Mrs Allard didn't seem to care for this side of the Blue Mountains.' Mr Watts grinned as he said this, as if he did not care much for Mrs Allard. Despite the difference in their stations, he was on good terms with Kershaw, and the two men shared certain plans for Christopher's future.

'Still coming to work for me, Chris, when you're old enough?' he asked then, turning to the child.

Christopher, dumb with relief, nodded. This was something which had been arranged over his head, and he was not sure whether he liked the idea. His father was determined that young Christopher was going to learn about sheep so that he could go out west and take up land and make a fortune.

The days of childhood seemed long, but the years passed quickly, and just after his fourteenth birthday he was packed off to Mr Watts' homestead to commence learning the business of being a flockmaster, and thus ultimately fulfilling his father's dream that he should take up land somewhere out there beyond the horizon in the New Country. The day of straight land grants, huge ones for silvertails like the Allards, and little ones for men who had come out under hatches like Jonathon Kershaw, had gone. There was some land for sale in the settled areas near towns, but most of this enormous country, from Cape York Peninsula in the tropics to Port Phillip near the chilly Bass Straits, was available for grazing purposes at a small rental paid direct to the Crown.

Christopher left home reluctantly. Trying to sound manly, he told his little sister to look after her mother and not forget to feed the hens as she usually did, being only four years old. Joanna was a pretty roly-poly of a child, with chestnut curls and her mother's fine dark eyes. She was atrociously spoiled, and Jonathon Kershaw, who would have put his son over his knee and thrashed him for half the things she did, became helpless under her mischievous gaze.

It did not take the lad long to realise that he much preferred cows and hens to sheep, but not having the heart to disappoint his father, he stuck it out with animals which he considered were the silliest and most boring beasts in all creation. As well, he became aware of the mental deterioration which seemed to be the lot of shepherds.

Most of these were former petty

criminals, men of a low and often stupid mentality, who, forced into a lonely existence with a few hundred sheep under their care, frequently became quite eccentric. It was the practice to refer to them as 'hatters', this title being derived from their habit, in coastal regions, of weaving hats from the leaves of the cabbage-tree palm, to pass the time and earn a little extra money. Now 'hatter' had come to mean a person mentally deranged.

'If that's what happens to a cove if he lives with sheep, I want none of it,' he said to George Forster one evening, about three years after leaving home.

George was two years older than Christopher, and had arrived a few months before to become what was later to be called a jackeroo. That is, he actually lived with Mr Watts and his family whilst learning the art of managing a sheep run. George was a little different from the run of young men in this position, as he was no 'Jacky Raw' out from Britain, but a native like Christopher. His father had been exiled for forgery many years before, and had become a man of wealth and importance back in Sydney. However, as the long-suffering wife who had loyally followed him into exile was extremely fecund, George had to make his own way in the world.

As Christopher soon discovered, George was lively, intelligent, reasonably well-educated, and despite a local lack of opportunity, had a keen instinct for winkling out chances of indulging in loose living.

'Well, Chris, if this damned drought goes on much longer, there won't be any sheep left to worry about,' replied George, looking out across a parched brown landscape dimming in the brief twilight of midsummer. 'And when that happens, me lad, it's back to Sydney for me.' He laughed meaningly. 'More girls in Sydney than out here.'

'Chris,' said Mr Watts, coming upon young Kershaw a few days later, 'how'd you like to go to South Australia?'

The youth nearly jumped out of his skin as his employer approached, for he had expected something different. The previous evening, he had allowed himself to be inveigled by George Forster into visiting a certain grog shanty in the district, and he half expected to be given his marching orders.

'South Australia, sir?' he stammered.

South Australia, the central slice of the continent, and only recently colonised, was hundreds of miles away.

'I'm sending some of the cattle from the River Lachlan station across to Adelaide. This drought could go on for ever, and there's a ready market for cattle in South Australia.'

'Yes, I'll go, Mr Watts.' He was so relieved not to be given a telling-off that he would have volunteered to go to the moon. Later in life, he realised that Mr Watts had seized this opportunity of separating young Christopher Kershaw from that bad influence, George Forster.

'Keep your eye open for a bit o' land you can take up,' advised his father before his son set forth, and Christopher, who had been happy at the prospect of escaping from sheep for a few months, felt the woolly beasts pressing in about him again.

2

News had come back to New South Wales that for those overlanding stock to Adelaide, the longest route was the shortest. The River Murray, for a great part of the journey from its source in the mountains on the eastern seaboard, flows west across level country, winding and looping backwards and forwards, but about ninety miles north-east of Adelaide it turns due south to eventually spend itself in the brackish waters of Lake Alexandrina. On the map, the shortest way to Adelaide appeared to be across the land contained within this angle, but the area lacked good water, so, having reached the River Murray, the overlanders did not venture further from its banks than necessary to graze the stock. In this country, the rate of regrowth was so slow that the tracks of earlier parties were easy to find and follow, but it was soon discovered that this was a mixed blessing, as the cattle had to be moved further out to find food, and zigzagged back to the river to be watered.

In charge of the expedition, with its several hundred head of cattle, was Mr Watts' nephew, Arthur Ellis, a superior young man not long out from England. The overseer, a Scot, was not much older, but vastly more experienced in bush life. Then there was an assortment of prisoners still working out their time, two men from the Hebrides who spoke Gaelic to each other, a trio who had come out 'legally' but were now free men, and in the minority, a pair of natives, Christopher Kershaw and a middle-aged man called Hughie Deane. These last were promptly dubbed Young Cornstalk and Old Cornstalk respectively.

For the first few weeks, the journey was gruelling but dull. They encountered only a few aboriginals, although there were many times when they were aware of the blacks' near presence, and signs, such as old campfires and trees with ovals of bark cut away to make crude canoes, were plentiful. At one place, Christopher, riding a little wide of the rest of the party, was startled to come across what he thought was part of a skull. However, the strange white object turned out to be a sort of cap fashioned from gypsum, and Hughie Deane informed him that this strange headgear was worn by women in mourning.

Near the South Australian border, trouble flared up for the first time, at the junction of the Murray and Rufus rivers. The Rufus is actually a short channel connecting the Murray to a large, brackish lake, and before white settlement, the banks, thick with reeds, were a favourite nesting place for a myriad waterfowl. The surrounding country being sandy and inhospitable, the Rufus River tribesmen were jealous of their hunting rights, and attempts by their neighbours to seize this rich source of food had made them hostile towards interlopers.

Firstly, they showed their displeasure by firing the scanty grass which Mr Ellis saw as food for his cattle. For the whites, there followed a frantic hour of shifting the beasts from danger, and rounding up the strays, all the while keeping an eye on the blacks, who had gathered on a nearby sandy ridge to watch the fun. It was nightfall before order was restored, with the cattle lowing restlessly and hungrily, but safely under guard.

At one of the watching posts, Christopher sat with Hughie Deane, bone tired, but trying to stay alert by drinking black tea from the quart pot. At the same time, Deane cooked a sort of pancake called jump bread in a frying pan. None of the others had much respect for his skill in making this dish, for they all swore that after partaking of it, a man was so weighted down that he was in no danger of falling from his horse.

Christopher had formed the opinion that Hughie Deane was the worst liar he had ever met, or was likely to meet, with his far-fetched tales of the very early days. Old Cornstalk had been born near Sydney in the year 1790, and was full of fantastic yarns about living with the blacks for a while, and actually crossing the Blue Mountains along the aboriginal trail a year before Mr Wentworth and his companions had found the proper way where the road was built. Still, Hughie Deane was entertaining, and his stories, added to the impromptu concerts held round the campfires of a night, helped fill in the hour before bedtime.

There were no songs or tall stories tonight, for everyone was tense, waiting for attack.

After a while, the youth stood up and paced about in the small area of light about the flames. The mosquitoes were voracious and persistent, and he hoped to discourage them by moving about. Almost immediately, he pitched forward on his face, as something resembling a thunderbolt hit him in the right shoulder. There was a flood of blistering language from Hughie Deane, followed by a series of yells, then shots and confusion, while Christopher lapsed into unconsciousness as he lay stickily in a growing pool of his own blood.

Later, he learned that Deane had thrown his jump bread at the savage rushing in to finish off his victim with a heavy hardwood waddy. The glutinous mass stuck itself to the painted skin, burning deeply, and sending the black man bounding off in agony.

Mr Ellis, as leader of the party and the one with the responsibility, cut the haft of the spear as close as he could to the wound, and tried to work out the serrated point without irreparably tearing the muscle. To ease the pain, they filled the lad up with rum, but after probing fruitlessly, Mr Ellis was forced to admit that this was a job for a surgeon. For the time being, all they could do was make the patient as comfortable as possible, settling him in one of the drays, and packing blankets and empty flour sacks about him to mitigate the pain caused by the jolting of the vehicle as it lurched across the roadless land.

Old Cornstalk stayed with him, sponging Christopher's face to reduce the persistent fever which had developed, holding him firmly over the worst terrain, and muttering profanities which were at the same time words of comfort. Days of misery passed slowly, until the party reached the point where the river turned south. Here, after consultation with a local settler, the first they had encountered in several hundred miles, Mr Ellis decided to place the patient in a litter between two horses, and move ahead of the main body through the hills to Adelaide. He had been advised by the settler that a Dr Fenwick in Adelaide was a capable surgeon who had earned distinction at Waterloo and was the only man in the colony who could handle a mess like that.

Adelaide turned out to be a sad cluster of poor buildings near a miserable stream called the Torrens. This was the city which was to have been the capital of a New Utopia, and was, in the year 1839, bankrupt and wondering what on earth had happened to place it in such a sorry plight. Most of the male population was engaged in road work, or in the construction of public buildings, this being the only way of employing them, while poor Governor Gawler pondered by what miracle he could pay them when his own private funds ran out.

Near the Auction Mart, where so much ruinous speculation in land had taken place, Mr Ellis drew rein and enquired of a loiterer as to where Dr Fenwick's house might be found.

'Coo!' exclaimed a nearby small boy in a tone of breathless admiration. 'It's an *overlander*!'

At the same time listening to instructions concerning the whereabouts of Dr Fenwick's residence, Arthur Ellis felt a certain glow spreading through him. Tall, slender, handsome, and twenty-eight years of age, he was also conscious that he was attracting the attention of two young ladies who happened to be passing. In Adelaide, reduced to eating kangaroo meat in order to preserve the colony's small numbers of stock, those enterprising men who brought cattle across country from New South Wales were considered to be cast in a heroic mould. They even wore a uniform of sorts, loose jackets over red shirts, slightly battered wide-brimmed hats, and beards partly covering suntanned faces. It was with an effort that Mr Ellis remembered that his purpose here was to take young Kershaw to the doctor.

It was with mild surprise that Christopher opened his eyes the next day to find himself in this comfortable bed made up crisply with clean sheets

29

and a good linen pillow-slip with a frill about the edge under his head. He had been awake before, but with the excruciating pain in his shoulder eased and the perpetual jolting gone, he had concluded mistily that he had died, and had dozed off again, with the feeling that if this were being dead, it had a lot to recommend it.

'How good to see you awake!' The voice was low and cultured and feminine, and belonged to a fortyish lady, neatly dressed in a grey gown with a cameo brooch at the neck, and with her hair tucked out of sight under a lace cap. She had bright blue eyes and a fair skin starting to wrinkle, and a sweet, friendly air which was reassuring.

'Where am I?' he asked, faintly.

'You're in Adelaide, at Dr Fenwick's house. I'm Sophia Fenwick, his sister. Dr Fenwick operated on your shoulder last night and removed that horrid barb.'

Another two days passed before he was able to take stock of his surroundings, and by this time he had been visited by Mr Ellis, who had ridden out to meet the others and had now returned to Adelaide. Arthur Ellis had actually arrived the night before, but with all the family except Miss Fenwick absent at a musical evening, he had not lingered, but had gone on to the wild spree which was almost obligatory at the end of a hard overland trip. Now he had a slightly dissolute look which made him more romantic than ever, if the way the two eldest Fenwick daughters kept popping in and out to ask if the patient needed anything could be taken as an indication.

He told Christopher not to worry, but to stay on here until he was quite well, although of course he himself would be off back to New South Wales within the week. The doctor's oldest daughter, Estelle, who had come in with a fresh jug of barley water for the patient — he had not finished the last, but although the day was cool, one could not be too careful with barley water — sent Mr Ellis a melting and reproachful look as he said this. Then he added casually that there must be plenty of land going for a song in South Australia with things so depressed, and he thought he would bring back a mixed lot of sheep and cattle and set up not too far from Adelaide. Miss Estelle's face immediately lit up, and she fairly flew out of the room, no doubt to tell her sisters the good news.

Christopher began to sort out the Fenwick family. At first, there had seemed to be an unlimited number of them, but now he had reduced them to Dr and Mrs Fenwick, Miss Fenwick, and four girls. There were also two sons, but they had gone off to try farming. Dr Fenwick terrified him, although he owed his life to the doctor's skill. He was a stump-legged, permanently angry-looking man, as well he might be, having lost most of his capital in rash land speculation, and receiving the greater part of his patients' dues in eggs, vegetables, cut firewood and the like, all the while trying to support his family. When he examined Christopher's shoulder, he was gentle, but gave the impression that at any moment he would lose his temper and punch the sore place. He treated his sister like dirt, thought the youth, with his Sophie this, and Sophie that, and Sophie for heavens' sake, while poor Miss Fenwick fluttered and flushed.

Mrs Fenwick was quiet and aloof, and from what she let drop, Christopher gathered that this colonial venture was a very great comedown for her. He knew quite well that she both endured and despised him.

The eldest girl, Estelle, was about twenty, and the three others stepped down from there to Laurel who was fourteen. Both Estelle and Jane, the second girl, were enamoured of Mr Ellis, and every time they could find the opportunity, pestered Christopher for information about him. He could not help them much, having never been on close terms with his employer's nephew, but this did not deter them.

Louisa, the third girl, was the beauty of the family, and about his own age. As he mended, he spent his days with his neck craned in the direction of the window, which looked out across the back yard, in the hope of glimpsing her as she took her turn with the outdoor chores.

Mr Ellis came again the day before leaving for home.

'It's arranged you can stay here until you're quite recovered,' he said, breezily. 'Then you may be able to join up with a party returning to New South Wales, if you don't decide to stay on here.' With this, he put out his hand to Christopher, before realising that the other's right arm was held firmly in a sling. Therefore, he could do no more than give a quick, manly squeeze to the left member lying limply on the turned-back sheet.

'Tell my parents I'm safe.'

'Of course.'

Hughie Deane visited him too, terribly ill at ease in the neatly furnished, spotlessly clean bedroom with lace curtains at the window, and a white linen runner on the chest of drawers. The lanky drover stood there in his rough bushman's clothes, hanging on to his dreadful old hat, not even daring to sit down. There were no racy reminiscences today, merely platitudes about hoping that Young Cornstalk would be better soon.

'Thanks for looking after me,' said Christopher, which made the other cringe more than ever, twirling his hat about in his fingers, and muttering in his grey-streaked beard. 'I hope you'll go and tell my Pa and Ma I'm all right if you get back as far as Bathurst.'

Old Cornstalk reckoned he wouldn't be going much further than Wagga Wagga down on the Murrumbidgee, but he would send word up to Bathurst through people he knew. Somehow, this was more reassuring than Mr Ellis's glib promises.

Recovering strength was a dull business, and even those fleeting glimpses of the lovely Louisa offered little compensation. If anything, they increased Christopher's melancholy frame of mind, for this stay with the Fenwicks was pointing up his many deficiencies.

There was reading, for instance. His parents had not been educated much past the signing of their own names, and he was little better. Mrs Watts, his employer's wife, had taken an interest in the younger boys working on the property, and had tried to help them with a little schooling, but after a day commencing at dawn and lasting until well past dark, Christopher seldom felt like applying himself to lessons in his scanty spare time.

It had been galling to admit to the Fenwicks that he could barely read. Instead of books, they brought in a tray and some cards, and he played patience with his good hand until he was thoroughly bored with the game. Laurel, or Laurie, as her aunt called her, came to the rescue. She loved reading aloud, she declared. It was quite her favourite pastime, and so, with her aunt sitting to one side stitching at the endless household sewing, she entertained the patient for hours on end.

Privately, he made up his mind that as soon as he was out of here, he would do something about learning to read properly. Until now, he had thought of book learning as something quite useless. He could manage all right if he needed to put his mark on anything, and that was all a cove like him would ever want. Having book learning was the equivalent of putting on airs, and even George Forster, who had attended the best school Sydney had to offer, never let himself be caught reading anything but the occasional newspaper.

This stay with the Fenwicks had given him an entirely different point of view. The stories little Miss Laurel read out were even better than the yarns he had heard spun about a campfire of a night. That one now about the fellow who was stranded on a desert island all those years — at the part where the faithful dog died of old age, Christopher had had to look away quickly so that the Misses Laurel and Sophia would not see the tears glistening in his eyes, because it so reminded him of the pain he had experienced at the age of twelve when a beloved dog had died.

He had to admit to himself, though, that reading a book himself would not be quite the same as listening to little Laurie Fenwick. She could change her voice to suit the different characters, and when she went all deep and lordly to impersonate the wicked Norman baron in *Ivanhoe*, he laughed so much that his healing shoulder threatened to open up again.

Physically, she was short for her age, too plump, with very fair curls, fine grey eyes with unexpectedly dark lashes, and a quick smile. Her sisters, with the unkind realism of close relatives, called her Dumpling, and Christopher thought it a shame that she did not control her appetite, because she was a nice-natured little soul. It was just as well, on those mild, autumnal afternoons when they sat out of doors, that he did not notice the quick fury in her eyes as he gazed in hopeless admiration after Louisa.

On the day that he managed a short stroll along North Terrace, where the Fenwick house was located, he realised that his stay was almost at an end and that he had to think about his return to New South Wales. Terrace was actually a very grand title for this thoroughfare, with its little houses dotted intermittently along the southern side, and a wide reserve, intended for gardens, but used for grazing animals, on the other. This open space extended well past the Torrens, the town's main water supply, and he could see past an untidy blacks' camp to a hillock, stripped bare of trees, where a public hanging had taken place in a picnic atmosphere not so long before.

The most attractive feature of the place, he decided, was a backdrop of ranges to the east, the foothills green after the first rains, and the higher tiers dark with forest. The sight of the mountains made him homesick.

That afternoon, while Dr Fenwick examined the almost healed scar, Christopher brought up the subject of payment for all this good treatment.

'Don't worry about it,' said the doctor, gruffly. 'I told 'em you'd be laid up about six weeks, and you've nothing to worry about in that respect.'

'You mean Mr Ellis paid . . . '

'No. The man Deane arranged everything.'

Christopher, buttoning his shirt, stared at him in astonishment, and the older man appeared embarrassed. Dr Fenwick hated talking about money, but when one was as hard up as he was, and someone paid him twenty pounds cash to board a patient, he did not argue. Young Kershaw was aghast. Poor Old Cornstalk! He hated to think how much of the old coot's savings had gone into this, and savings were hard to come by on eleven shillings a week and keep.

You'd have thought Mr Ellis would have arranged it, he told himself. Him and all his grand airs! It was his responsibility, for there was no question of being in debt to the boss when one was so badly hurt working for that boss. Owing money to Hughie Deane was a different cup of tea.

He would have to try to save up and repay Hughie when he ran up against him again.

It took away the joy of getting better.

3

'Why are you crying, Ma?' Christopher held his mother at arm's length, scarcely able to believe that he was actually home after all this time.

'Because I'm so happy. I've been that worried, Chris, thinkin' you was dead out somewhere in the bush, with no proper marker on your grave, or fallen in with bad company, or — oh, I'm so glad to see you!'

He clasped the slight woman to him again, while his sister Joanna danced and squealed about them until told by her mother, between bursts of laughter and tears, to fetch her father.

'Stop it, Ma!' Christopher commanded, with all the wonderful confidence of his nineteen years. 'I can look after myself.'

Then his father came, almost entirely grey-haired now, a quiet, powerful man well into his middle years, who took his son's hand gravely and said nothing more than that he was glad to see him home.

At first, Christopher and his mother did most of the talking, she afire with questions as to how he had spent the last two years, while Joanna, tall for her age and already with a hint of beauty to come in her freckled face, listened with wide, dark eyes. To her, this brother who had been away for such a long time was a god-like creature of great age and maturity: another decade would elapse before she could meet him on the common ground of adulthood.

When his family had had their fill of his adventures, they told him the local news. It had been a bad two years for many, although the Kershaws had managed very well, having never owed a penny to a soul, even though it meant pinching and scraping and going without at times. Their creek had not run dry, so that they had not had to sell their stock to the boiling-down works like some. Many settlers who had taken up small farms in the area had been forced to give up and go back to Sydney, to find some sort of work to tide them over, while Mr Watts, who had seemed so rich and solid, had been deeply in debt to the banks and had lost everything. His nephew, Arthur Ellis, had taken stock from the Lachlan River station and had overlanded again to Adelaide to set up there on his own. Mr Watts, however, was staying on at his former establishment, because the new owner had kept him on as manager for the time being, which was a comedown after being the most important man in these parts.

'Do you think they'd take me on again?' Obviously, his parents had managed very well without him all this time, even to hiring men as required, and he would have to find work if he wanted to stay in the district.

Jonathon Kershaw looked uncomfortable, and in the dim light of the lamp Chris saw his parents exchange glances.

'Captain Allard — the man I was assigned to when I was sent out — well, he's the one what's bought out Mr Watts and I'm telling you straight, Chris, I don't like the notion of you going to work for him.'

'I see, Pa.' Christopher saw it all very plainly. There was something degrading about going cap in hand to the man who had been master when his father had been a prisoner. 'Is George Forster still there?'

'No place for him any more. The two oldest Allard lads are with Mr Watts, learning how to run things, but the Captain took George back with him to his place at Liverpool to work there. George called in a few times to ask if we'd heard anything of you. He kindly read out those letters you'd sent us.'

While his father was speaking, Christopher was conscious that more glances were passing between his parents, and unbidden, the memory returned of two little boys in tasselled caps, and murmurs in the night betwixt husband and wife as they spoke of Captain Allard in low, secret voices.

'In that case,' he said, slowly, 'I'll have to think about what I'm going to do.'

There was one thing he knew he was going to do, he pondered later, as he lay down on his bed in the lean-to room, and that was something about his sister. Surely there was a school in Bathurst where she could have some of those rough edges smoothed away? The time he had spent with the Fenwick family had left an indelible impression, and he was now apt to compare other girls and women unfavourably with Louisa, the goddess and unattainable beauty, with her graceful carriage, and clear, soft diction. If little Joanna ended up with only one-quarter of Louisa's ladylike attributes, he would be satisfied.

His parents were not rich, nor were

they dirt poor, these days. What had struck him first as he rode up that morning was that the place had a well-ordered and neat air about it, as if his father could dip into his purse when necessary. The old bark roof had been replaced by wooden shingles, a room had been added, there were curtains at the windows and sheets on the beds, and Jo wore decent clothes instead of the dungarees which had been his lot as a child. They could certainly afford to have their only daughter schooled beyond a little reading and writing.

As for finding work, he could manage for several weeks.

He had a few pounds saved, for one unexpected benefit of his self-imposed task of improving his reading ability was that he had something to do in his scanty spare time besides playing cards and drinking in the dirty hovels which passed for inns out in the bush.

His father lost no time in speaking to him again about buying up some sheep while prices were still low, and looking about for suitable land.

Sheep, thought Christopher. Damned sheep. It looks like sheep for me whether I want it or not, with Pa going on talking about how he has a little put away, and me being nearly twenty and old enough to be setting up on my own, and when the seasons were good, there was nothing like sheep for coining money, and provided a cove was sensible and did not throw his blunt around and did not let himself get into the clutches of the banks, he could end up a rich man.

The young man thought of all the things one had to worry about with sheep, getting enough shepherds, the scab, footrot, sudden frosts killing off the lambs, crows coming down and picking out their eyes, the occasional ones speared by wild blacks and the resultant strife, the worms, the scouring, the dust and burrs in the wool, and the silly way the brutes had of all of a sudden leaping, one after the other, into the air as if they were actually jumping over something solid. Then he knew, with an enormous conviction, that he detested sheep with every part of his being, and that he could not bear the idea of spending the rest of his life with them.

Still, neither could he at this time bear to hurt his father's feelings, so he settled down to enjoy his stay at home, without worrying too much about the future, and before he had quite realised it, two months had slipped past.

There was a ball in Bathurst to celebrate the young Queen's birthday during May, and judging by the horses and conveyances tethered along the street as Christopher rode towards the hall, everyone who was anyone in the district was attending. Young Joanna had a cold, which kept his parents at home, but they had urged him not to miss the ball on their account, and as he had a natural longing for company his own age, he had been quite agreeable.

Christopher joined the throng of

bashful young men inside the hall, they being dressed, like himself, in their self-conscious best. The local gentry were dancing at their end of the hall, plainly indicated by the floorboards there being waxed, while the common herd had to make do with an unpolished surface, although judging by the frisky way some of the girls were being twirled about, it did not much matter. There were far more men than women present, and although some of the ladies at the gentry's end were sitting out, it was not *done* to ask them, so during the first part of the evening Christopher managed only three dances.

However, he met up with some old friends, and they went along the street to a public-house and had a couple of glasses. He related his own experiences working his way back from South Australia, and in return they warned him about the young Allards, whose wild ways would have landed them in trouble with the law if they had been of less exalted station.

Back at the dances, having missed out on a partner, Christopher was standing by a wall watching the others when he felt a tug at his sleeve. Glancing back, he saw a ginger-headed girl, who was dressed skittishly in a dress patterned with pink and white checks and embellished with frills and pieces of tatty ribbon, in a style about five years out of date. She was passably pretty, with pale blue eyes under thin brows, a turned-up nose, and a silly mouth above a receding chin. He knew her, of course. It was Millie Hooper, daughter of a local grog shanty keeper. Everyone knew Millie Hooper, or at least, all the men did, and the women pretended that they did not. One infant amongst the innumerable small Hoopers produced regularly by her mother was supposed to be Millie's child, and popular opinion had it that if there were not more, it was just good luck.

She was about four years older than Kershaw, and looking at her now, he hoped that she was not trying to make up to him.

'Remember me, Chris?' Millie sounded incredibly timid for a girl of her habits and reputation.

'Yes. How are you, Millie?' He sounded as offhanded as he could manage. After all, he had travelled, and he doubted whether Millie had been more than ten miles from Bathurst in all her life.

'Could you see me 'ome, Chris?'

'No,' he replied, bluntly, and then, seeing the stricken expression on her face, he added, 'I'm sorry, Millie, but I've got a girl.' This was a lie, for the secret daydreams he still carried about Louisa Fenwick could never be described as 'having a girl'.

'I don't mean like that, Chris. I just 'oped you'd take me, quick, on your horse. It's them Allards.' Her mouth started to tremble as if she were about to cry. 'I'm scared of them.'

He had already picked out the Allards, a handsome pair, both blond and tall and well built. The elder by a year, Stephen, had a perpetual sneer on his face, as if he had already discovered that the world was not to his liking, and although Percy, the younger, carried an air of weak amiability, he was plainly very much under his brother's thumb.

'I got a real sweetheart now, Chris, but 'e's away droving,' she added, and he made up his mind.

'Come on,' he said, yielding to a chivalry he would regret later.

'They got 'old of me a couple of weeks ago,' Millie explained, as he unhitched Blackie and helped the girl up before leaping on himself. 'I've never minded bein' nice to a fellow if I likes 'im, but they were real cruel. That younger one, Percy, wouldn't be so bad on 'is own, I reckon, but Steve's a real brute.'

'If they forced you, you should have gone to the constable.'

'Don't make me laugh, Chris. They're the Allards, and I'm just Millie 'Ooper. My word's nothin' against theirs.'

'You'd better marry this sweetheart of yours and get him to take you away to some place where no one knows you,' he advised.

''E won't be back for three months,' said Millie, and began to weep in a messy, sniffling fashion which irritated Christopher so much that he was glad when they reached the littered yard of her home.

She thanked him nicely, and he rode off quite unaware that he had gathered up enough trouble for himself to make the average man swear off good deeds for the rest of his life.

4

He was buying stores in Bathurst when the indiscretion of interfering between the Allards and their desires was brought home to him. He had loaded the dray, and was untethering the horse when a sneering, jeering voice cut across his thoughts.

'Look, Percy, if it ain't the currency lad who stole our currency lass from us!'

Naturally, he immediately turned and found himself face to face with Stephen Allard and his brother Percy. Although it was not much past noon, they had plainly spent some time in a public-house, and they had about themselves a wild and reckless aura which meant trouble.

'There's no accounting for it, is there, Percy?' continued Stephen, advancing with his hands thrust into the pockets of his well-cut riding breeches. 'Still, as they say, like calls to like, and I expect that's why our Millie prefers the son of a convict harlot to Exclusives like ourselves.'

Kershaw could not believe his ears. He rehitched Rupe to the post, and faced Stephen squarely.

'Mind what you say,' he countered, and with a shock, saw the intense hatred on the others' faces. It baffled him. No one in their right mind could work up emotion over a girl like Millie Hooper, but apparently the Allards were so used to having their own way that the slightest interference with their plans aroused their wrath. He could not credit that they were still carrying a grudge over the way he had insulted their caps all those years ago.

'Yes, I'll mind what I say,' said Stephen in the careful tones of the slightly drunk. 'I'll say you're the son of a convict harlot.'

Christopher lost his temper, flung himself at Stephen, and made the mistake of his life. He was quite able to hold his own in the average brawl, but this time his antagonist was a trained and accomplished boxer, and the next thing Christopher knew, he was lying on his back staring up at a piece of sky made circular by the ring of faces looking down at him. He scrambled to his feet, but one fist crashed on his ribs while another pummelled his head. He was on his back again, and as he struggled up, he felt the blood trickling hot across his mouth and down his chin. He was dizzy and winded, but still determined to punish Stephen. Fortunately for him, someone called out that the law was on its way, and Percy grabbed his brother's arm and pulled him away, leaving Kershaw standing in the middle of the road, muddied and bloodied, sore all over, and bewildered by the whole event.

An older man called Hargraves, a farmer whom he knew slightly, took him across to the horse trough outside a public-house. As he recovered, he unknotted the scarf he wore about his neck and used it as a makeshift towel.

'That young man has a nasty temper,' commented the farmer.

'And a filthy tongue,' muttered Christopher, putting his own tongue round his mouth to make sure that all his teeth were still there. One on the upper left side seemed a little loose, but otherwise the damage was mostly superficial. 'He couldn't say that about my mother, Mr Hargraves. It was because I helped a girl they were after a while back.' Then something occurred to him. 'I thought the constable was coming.'

'I said that, lad, to break it up. Now, if you feel up to handling your dray, I'll ride part of the way with you just in case that pair of young devils are waiting for you.'

Of course, he had to explain his battered appearance at home, but to spare any distress, he told a garbled story of how he had been set upon by a drunk, and having his pride, he made it sound as if he had come off better than he actually had, for he was under no illusions as to what would have happened if the fight had not broken up when it had. He would have been drubbed into an unconscious, bleeding heap.

Two days later, when his cuts and bruises were ceasing to hurt so badly, he was sawing logs over the pit with his father when he noticed an untidy, rather dirty, little man approaching. This bleary-eyed, ratty individual was Horrie Hooper, grog shanty keeper of dubious reputation, and Millie Hooper's father.

Christopher was puzzled, because Hooper was no friend of his father's, but he felt guilty too, because a long time ago, before he had gone overlanding to Adelaide, he had been sick on Mr Hooper's beaten-earth floor during a drinking session with George Forster. He preferred to forget that sort of thing.

'Well, young Chris,' smirked Hooper, 'it's good to see I'm gonna 'ave a son-in-law who don't mind soilin' 'is 'ands.'

Jonathon Kershaw stopped his sawing, and wiped his palms on his trousers before speaking, for his son was too stupefied to utter a sound.

'What's all this? I ain't heard my lad's thinking of getting married.'

'Well, if he ain't, 'e'd better afore Millie starts showin'.' Hooper grinned, showing a collection of gaps and broken teeth. 'Now, Mr Kershaw, you was sent out legal, same as me, so's I can talk to you, man to man. We 'ad to pretend the other brat was ours, and I'll say this for Millie, she ain't blowin' the gaff as to who's the father o' this one any more than t'other, but when a cove gits into a fight over a girl, you can't kid me he ain't nuts on 'er.'

For one crazed instant, Christopher wondered whether there had been some hideous fluke of nature which had delayed things for two and a half years, but then sense prevailed. Since he had come home, he had laid eyes on Millie only once, and he could not possibly be responsible for her condition.

'In case you're nervy,' continued Hooper, 'I've spoken to parson and 'e's expecting yer tomorrow mornin' to chat about the weddin' and git the licence fixed up.'

Christopher found his voice at last.

'But I don't want to marry Millie.'

'Ain't a matter o' wantin' to. You 'ave to.' Hooper had a monotonous whine in his voice as if he were forever begging favours. 'She's not a bad little thing, Millie ain't. She can cook real nice when she puts her mind to it.'

'Me and Chris wants to talk,' interrupted Jonathon Kershaw. 'You needn't worry. If there's been wrong done, it'll be put right.'

'Orright, orright,' muttered Hooper. 'I knew you'd see right done, Mr Kershaw. Now good day to you both.'

Briefly, Christopher was surprised at Hooper's repeated use of the term, 'Mr Kershaw'. His father had, as the shanty-keeper had pointed out, 'come out legal' like himself, but Hooper had never risen past his own level, and even at this time, conceded the older Kershaw a little respect.

When the visitor was well out of earshot, Jonathon, who continued stacking some of the wood they had sawn, spoke his mind.

'How could you have been such a bleeding fool? Millie's a dimwitted slut.'

'Pa, it's not me. It can't be. I ain't seen her but the once, about two weeks ago, at the Queen's Birthday Ball. She was scared of the Allards, and I saw her home, that's all.'

'Then why was you fighting over her?'

'I wasn't. I didn't tell you the truth about the fight. It was with Stephen Allard. He was half seas over, and said something about Ma. I wouldn't stand for it. You can ask Mr Hargraves. He was there.'

Jonathon Kershaw stared at him, his eyes, the colour of which he had handed on to his son, expressionless. Silently, he reached out and gripped the young man's shoulder.

'And a proper hiding he gave me,' added Christopher, unhappily. 'I don't understand it, Pa. It wasn't just over Millie. He acted as if he wanted to kill me.'

'That doesn't matter. You still did right. Now, first thing in the morning, you'd better saddle up and be off. We'll say you had a message about a droving job. Keep going, as far as you can get. I'll tell your mother the truth when you've gone.'

'What about Millie?'

'What about her? I'm not having that trash in my family.'

Christopher felt a swelling of love and gratitude towards his father, and briefly they were so close that he had the courage to ask what he had wanted to know for years.

'Pa, why did they transport you?'

His father wiped the blade of the saw with a rag, taking care as he performed the simple action.

'Less you know the better. But, lad, I get to thinkin' sometimes. You know grass trees?'

The youth was astounded, but he nodded. One saw grass trees everywhere one travelled, large, strange plants with great bunches of grass-like long leaves on short stumps, called by some blackboys, and by others yaccas.

'They spread by sending up shoots from their roots when things aren't right for them. They don't flower unless there's been a fire through. That's a lot like my life's been, Chris. I kept alive, but nothin' bloomed for me until I went through the fire. My past is past, lad. I've a farm, a good wife, a handsome son, and a pretty little daughter.'

Then he spoiled this intimacy by bringing up the subject of sheep again. If Chris had to go away from home,

Jonathon suggested, he might as well make the most of it. He could put up the blunt for Chris to buy some sheep and enough supplies to tide him over the first year if Chris found some land, say down in the Port Phillip District.

For Christopher, it was a moment of decision. He could accept his father's offer and give his life over to hated sheep, or he could make his own way. He knew quite well that if he accepted the latter choice, there would be no parental help forthcoming.

He refused.

Joanna bawled when she learned that her brother was leaving, but he told her to be a good girl and learn all she could so that they could write letters to each other.

'If there's any trouble with the young Allards,' Jonathon Kershaw told his son as he helped Christopher saddle Blackie in the frosty chill of dawn the next day, 'I'll send word to Old Flogger — Captain Allard. He's a hard man, but he's fair, and I reckon he owes me a favour still.'

'Him? A favour?' Christopher's astonishment was reflected in his voice, while at the same time he tried to make sense of it. Here were the Allard sons picking a fight with him, and here was Pa talking about favours owed by their father.

'Yes, him. Now go and kiss your mother. She's crying out her heart.'

There was a high point along the track leading from the farm, and here Christopher drew rein and turned in the saddle to gaze back towards his home. The sun was piercing through the mist, illuminating all in a peculiarly golden light. How peaceful and pretty it looked there, with its paddocks spreading lushly on either side of their stream, hung now with the willows his mother had planted from twigs someone had given her. He could remember, as a small child, when there had been only a cleared patch about a tiny hut, with the wild and inhospitable bush pressing in all around.

He blinked several times to clear the tears gathering under his lids, and then, resolutely, kicked Blackie forward with his heels.

5

A few weeks after his twenty-first birthday, Christopher rode into Adelaide. He had heard that there had been rich deposits of copper ore discovered north of Adelaide and that, consequently, labour was scarce and wages were up in South Australia.

The settlement on the plains between the wooded Mount Lofty Ranges and St Vincent's Gulf had improved considerably since his last visit. Its air of disillusionment, brought about by the misery of the first settlers as they suffered through mismanagement and the quarrels of those who were supposed to be displaying leadership, had given way to a more cheerful atmosphere as farms spread out from Adelaide's boundaries, and mineral discoveries in the hinterland promised wealth. Despite its raw newness, the capital had a pleasing order about it, a sense of being well-behaved reflected in the humblest smocked labourer. Instantly noticeable was an absence of that crude language and thieves' cant which grated upon the ears of visitors to New South Wales.

Christopher found a livery stable and left Blackie there, after enquiring as to where he might find cheap but decent lodgings. He took a room at a nearby inn, and tidied himself before setting out for a walk in what was to him a vast and noisy metropolis.

There had been a heavy fall of rain the previous week, but now the clear August sunshine had hardened the unpaved streets, and in the city blocks which did not yet boast buildings — and they were many — the vegetation grew clean and green. To match the springlike day, with its white woolly clouds strolling across the sky, the young ladies shopping in their pairs looked fresh and pretty. That was another thing about Adelaide. There was a higher proportion of females in ratio to the males than in the convict colonies, where decent girls were always in short supply.

Wandering along, he recalled, with an inward smile, his youthful adoration of Louisa Fenwick, that conceited young woman whose only topic of conversation seemed to be about the effect of the Australian climate upon her complexion. On the spur of the moment, he decided to call on the Fenwicks.

New houses had changed the appearance of the street, and after some indecision he paused in front of the Fenwicks' residence. It, too, had changed, being larger, and with its garden in a far more flourishing state than he remembered. A girl was tying a creeper against the picket fence, and misled by memory and family resemblance, he thought at first that it was Louisa.

She was a most attractive girl, with silver-blonde hair drawn to the crown and arranged in ringlets on either side of her face, a dear little straight nose and a wide mouth which looked as if it needed little excuse to make it open in laughter. She wore an everyday brown gown, covered by a practical apron, but in spite of this, it was easy to see that her waist was delicately formed beneath a high little bust. She must have sensed that someone was staring at her, because she straightened up and turned to face Christopher as he stood gaping over the fence.

For her part, she saw a loose-knit young man of a little under six feet in height, kept lean by the hard life of the bush. He was very suntanned, and the hair revealed as he awkwardly removed his hat was brown, a little bleached by the sun, and slightly wavy. His features were fairly regular, and his visage was pleasant without being strikingly handsome. His eyes were hazel, on the dark side, with long, almost girlish eyelashes, which he detested.

'Why! Mr Kershaw!'

For an instant, he wondered whom she was addressing, for she was the first person who had called him 'Mr Kershaw' in a very long time, if ever. He had recognised her by now. She was little Laurel Fenwick, the girl her sisters had nicknamed 'Dumpling'. Since he had seen her last, she had grown up three inches and had lost at least a stone, with the wonderful results he saw before him.

'Hullo,' he said, in a mumble. He did not dare call her 'Laurie', as he had when she was a fourteen-year-old child. Everything about her made him feel impossibly uncouth. She was so pretty and so refined and so sweetly spoken that he was almost struck dumb.

'This is a wonderful surprise! We never thought to see you again!' she exclaimed, laying aside string and scissors.

Then she approached the gate, while he grasped his hat in confusion and tried to think of something to say. With every second that passed, she grew more beautiful and desirable, and within three minutes he was hopelessly in love and feeling absolutely miserable about it.

'Do come in, Mr Kershaw,' she invited. 'We take tea at this time, and Mother and the others will be delighted to see you.'

He had had some thoughts of having a few drinks and seeking out female entertainment in the usual way of bushmen in town, but now the idea became quite repulsive to him in its coarseness. Soon, he found himself in the Fenwicks' prim little drawing-room, clutching a cup of incredible delicacy, and nibbling bread and butter, while the ladies of the house made polite conversation. He felt ill at ease amidst the good furniture the Fenwicks had shipped out from England, and which looked almost as out of place as he did in this small stone and *pisé* house.

Mrs Fenwick was still aloof, but Miss Sophia, the doctor's sister, was as friendly as ever. He soon gathered that the two eldest girls were now married. Mr Ellis had returned to South Australia as he had promised, and was now Estelle's husband and running a property about fifty miles north of Adelaide. The second girl, Jane, had wed a coffee-shop owner, and the Fenwicks, Christopher understood, were not pleased about this. Sheep or coffee, it was a way of earning a living, but here, as in New South Wales, sheep had the higher social value.

Louisa was still at home, and a disappointment. True, she was lovely to look at, but now had that slightly disagreeable expression of a young woman who had discovered that the world did not share her high opinion of herself. However, he found it hard not to stare at Laurie.

They enquired, politely, about his plans, and he made a vague reply. The truth was, he had no plans, except to take a brief spell from droving.

'You must return one evening and see my brother,' insisted Miss Sophia, as he took his leave. He could not help noticing that Mrs Fenwick did not press the invitation and he felt that he understood her point of view. He was not their kind. But as he said goodbye, he saw the imploring question in Laurie's grey eyes, and he felt the blood pounding in his body. If he had a scrap of sense, he knew, he should mount his horse and ride out of Adelaide on the morrow, but he would not.

Laurie felt the same way as he did, and damn it all, he would see her again.

After this, he gave up the notion of going out on the spree, and instead found a bookseller's store, where he invested a few shillings in a couple of volumes, the contents of which, he hoped, would make him appear a little less ill-educated.

Finding employment in Adelaide proved to be no problem at all, for the next morning, on going to the stables to attend to his horse,

Christopher was approached by the owner who asked whether the young man would consider working for him, as he seemed to know a lot about horses. Nothing could have suited the lovesick New South Welshman more, and he accepted immediately.

Two evenings later, he presented himself to Dr Fenwick, who at first was delighted to see this living evidence of one of his more spectacular cures. Within half an hour, his enthusiasm waned as he realised that his youngest daughter was far more interested in the visitor than she should have been. The next day, Miss Sophia arrived at the stables, and after a little probing with such leading questions as didn't he think Laurie had turned into a beautiful young lady, she told him straight out that he had better not call at the house again. Her brother had very rigid ideas about those with whom his daughters came in contact, and had promised to show Mr Kershaw the door if he dared enter the house again.

It was crushing, but Miss Sophia, behind her air of fluttering helplessness, had a surprisingly devious mind.

'Laurie and I,' she said, 'frequently walk along North Terrace, on fine afternoons. We always prefer to walk in an easterly direction.'

He did not need it spelled out to him, and horses from the stables began taking exercise along North Terrace at that same time, although they must have been both bored and puzzled as they were led along at an ambling rate while their mentor spoke to a young lady. Miss Sophia always trailed a discreet five yards behind, and these meetings were repeated several times.

At night, Christopher allowed his fancies to run away, to the possibility of marriage and taking her back to New South Wales with him. Surely his father, who had spoken of having something put away, could help them to set up house.

He no longer had to worry about Millie Hooper. A letter, written by a friend of his father's, had informed him that Millie's sweetheart had turned up in the nick of time to make her an honest woman. It was harder to dispose of other problems.

Asking his father for help would be a matter of giving in all the way, which meant sheep.

Then, if he went back to Bathurst, he ran the risk of encountering the Allards, and enemies of that calibre could make life impossible for him and a delicately nurtured young wife. As he had many times before, he tried to work out why Stephen and Percy hated him so much. There was something there not quite right, nothing he could put a finger to, but compounded of half-heard whispers, coming through a thin wall long ago when his parents had seen Captain Allard in Bathurst and he had derided the Allard boys. The greatest puzzle was his father's extraordinary claim that Captain Allard, 'Old Flogger', owed him a favour. Was it in some way connected with the state of modest but solid comfort in which his parents now lived? No, it couldn't be. Pa wouldn't take favours from the man to whom he had been in bond while serving out his time.

Pa's talk about the favour simply did not make sense against the inexplicable hatred held for Christopher by the two eldest Allard sons.

The meetings with Laurie continued, and he knew that any day someone would report back to her parents. Oddly, it was Laurie, who had been gently raised and should have known better, who made the suggestion which led to disaster.

The Fenwicks as a family retired early, and were sound sleepers. Therefore, why should she not creep out after the candles were snuffed and meet him?

'We can't do that!' he protested, not very sincerely, thinking that at last he could take her in his arms.

'Why? How else are we going to be together?'

Together? What did she mean by

that? No, he must not think such things. Laurie was a sweet innocent, and he must not take advantage of her youthful inexperience.

'But if your parents find out . . . '

'They won't, Kit. They sleep like logs. About ten o'clock tonight, behind the stables.'

Stables sounded very grand. The structure, on vacant ground next to the Fenwicks' house, comprised one horse box, one compartment for the dry storage of hay and so forth, and a partly walled extension to shelter Dr Fenwick's small carriage, a locally constructed hybrid designed to take him safely over rough tracks.

So, he waited in the chilly gloom behind the stables, until, after what seemed an endless interval of darkness, she flitted through the shadows into his arms. It should have been very romantic, but the stables had, well, an odour, and the horse whinnied so loudly in the middle of their first kiss that both nearly jumped out of their skins. As well, Christopher was overwhelmed by shyness.

She was so perfect, with her tiny body, her fair ringlets, her sweetly chiselled features and soft voice, and he was only a rough bushman. The Millie Hoopers of the world would have been lolling back on the hay, half undressed and pulling him down to them within three minutes, but Laurie sat stiffly at his side, cold and nervous. He could not guess that she was afire with emotions she did not understand, and that she longed for him to embrace her until she half swooned. The heroines in the novels she enjoyed always did this in the arms of their lovers, and she accepted it as normal. Laurie did not have the faintest idea of what went on between males and females in private.

'You're cold,' he whispered, finding his tongue, and taking one of her hands in his.

'A little.'

Then:

'What's that?'

They both strained their ears. A horse had cantered along North Terrace, had been drawn to a halt outside the Fenwick house, and now they could hear the knocker crashing against the front door, and, after a pause, voices.

'Someone wants Father.'

'We'd best go, then.'

'But I can't if they're up. They'll want to know where I've been.'

He was about to tell her to say that she'd been out to the privy when he realised that this excuse would not work. She was fully dressed. She should have been in her night attire.

'Well, we'll stay here quietly until all the fuss is over.'

'But Father rides Bess on night calls. He doesn't drive in the dark. And the saddle's hanging up there.'

It was, practically over their heads.

'Quick, before he comes, then!'

They were too late. Dr Fenwick, with uncounted years of night calls and hasty dressing behind him, was already running across the yard, pulling on his coat and somehow holding his bag at the same time. During the past half-hour, a full moon had risen above the high ridges of the ranges to the east, so that as they tried to slip away behind the building, the guilty pair were revealed.

For a man whose usual behaviour tended to the choleric, the doctor was very calm, and this seemed more alarming than any manifestation of rage.

Dr Fenwick was a firm believer in a world with all in their predestined places. One of the things which had prompted him into migrating were changes back in Britain, with workers spouting democracy and other dangerous heresies. Unfortunately, again and again, he had come up against examples of impudent ways in the lower classes right here in South Australia. Until this moment, he had neither liked nor disliked Christopher. The young man was a healthy specimen of the working class, a rural toiler of the type necessary in this huge new country. Despite the felonry of his parents, the boy seemed to be living honestly, which Dr Fenwick had been told was quite frequent with the children of convicts, and in the fullness of time he would marry some little maidservant who would produce many young Kershaws to till the soil, herd the cattle, drive wagons, build houses, and generally provide a foundation for civilised society.

While Dr Fenwick stood grappling with his thoughts, Laurie began crying, and Christopher placed a protective arm about her slim shoulders.

'Dr Fenwick, sir, I know what you're thinking, but . . .'

'Get out!'

'But, sir, I want to marry Laurie.'

'Marry my daughter! You!' The outraged father was recovering himself. 'Laurel, go into the house. Immediately! I've a dying man waiting, and I'll talk to you when I return. As for you, you young guttersnipe, get out of my sight!'

6

The man sitting under the veranda on that hot February pre-dawn of 1851 could afford a wry smile over the fiasco of his romance with Miss Laurel Fenwick. Basically, it was the reason why he had come to Melbourne, and now found himself in his present bad position, with foreclosure and bankruptcy imminent.

When he had come ashore at the landing place below the freshwater falls on the Yarra Yarra, his feelings had been a mixture of hope that he would somehow make good here and be able to send for Laurie, and sheer relief at having dry and steady land under his feet again. What had happened after Dr Fenwick had caught his daughter with her sweetheart was, to Christopher, just another example of the mysterious power people of social standing held, regardless of whether they were wealthy or not.

Dr Fenwick was not a rich man, but in Adelaide he was a person of standing, and as such, was able to make sure that young Kershaw was banished. He simply made it clear to Christopher's employer that some of his customers would go elsewhere if he kept on the young man, and Christopher was sufficiently intelligent to understand that this would probably happen again.

So, with regret, he sold his only asset, Blackie, to a lady who wanted a quiet mount for riding about town. He and Blackie had shared much, hard times and adventures, and it was a real wrench to stroke her dark nose for the last time.

He kept his saddle, and carrying this and the small bag of his personal belongings, he trudged up the hill past the warehouses, ducking his head to protect his face from the stinging, squall-driven rain blowing in from the south-west. Inside his bag was a passionate letter from Laurie, left at his lodgings by, he suspected, that feather-brained romanticist Miss Sophia. This letter not only declared her undying love and full-hearted acceptance of his proposal of marriage, but on a more practical level, gave him an address to which he could safely write, and again he suspected that Miss Sophia had arranged this. In retrospect, he wondered whether Miss Sophia had been the one to suggest their disastrous night rendezvous.

It goes to show, he thought many times, what wild ideas are rushing about inside the heads of some of these milk-and-water spinsters.

Despite the rain, and the suspicion that several sneezes heralded a cold, he could see that Melbourne, like that other town nearly five hundred miles behind him, had improved since his last visit. True, pigs, hens and the odd cow still roamed the crabholed main streets, and cabbages grew on town lots which had exchanged hands at grossly inflated prices only a few years before. The early Melburnian, like the Adelaide pioneers, no sooner arrived than they were seized by grandiose notions concerning their settlement's future. This had resulted in reckless gambling in land prices, and when coupled with generally depressed conditions in the early forties, had led to a crash which left many a would-be tycoon contemplating pauperhood. Still, by 1843, the more prudent had settled in solidly, and although destitute migrants still camped wretchedly along the swampy banks of the river, there were respectable buildings in the main part of the town.

Christopher tramped up Elizabeth Street, an euphemism for what out of town would have been termed a washaway, for after heavy rain it ceased being a street and became a stream. He skirted a group of aboriginals sitting at the intersection of Elizabeth and Collins streets, and this being the lowest point in the latter east-to-west thoroughfare, he stood for a few moments trying to decide which direction to take, choosing east. He had gone only a few yards when a hand descended upon his right shoulder, which was twinging a little as it had in damp weather ever since that spear hit it, and he nearly jumped out of his skin.

'Hullo! Fancy seeing you here!' boomed a hearty voice, and turning, Christopher saw a stocky, solid young man wearing a beaver hat on black curly hair above a pale, round face framed with matching dark sidewhiskers.

It was, of course, his old friend George Forster, but George looked so different in a good dark frock coat above buff trousers instead of the shabby, out-of-elbow riding clothes which had been his uniform at Mr Watts' place, that it took Christopher a few seconds to orientate.

'What are you doing here?' he demanded.

'Doing? I live here. Come round the corner to my place, and tell me why *you're* here.' So saying, George took the other's arm, and steered him towards 'my place', which was a neat stone-and-timber hostelry. As they progressed thither, Christopher noticed that George had not lost his eye for the girls, judging by the way his greenish-grey gaze roved hither and yon to take in ladies out shopping.

George soon filled him in on the story of his success. Sensing that the drought could not last for ever, and not liking his situation with Captain Allard, he had bought up sheep cheaply. He drove them south, and had the good fortune to meet up with a new chum, fresh out from the Old Country, who had taken up a lease and was in the market for stock.

George had made an excellent profit, and came down across the ranges to Melbourne with the idea of spending it all on a spree. However, as he had ridden into town, he had realised that this isolated settlement on the northern bank of the Yarra Yarra must be the thirstiest spot on earth. He was not a hundred yards along Elizabeth Street before his horse, unused to civilisation, had tripped over a heap of bottles left in the middle of the road by roisterers.

This set George to thinking deeply. He could waste the money in the belt against his skin by adding to those bottles, or he could profit from the insatiable thirsts of others. Thus, he concluded, leading his friend into a snug little parlour with a fire blazing in the grate, he was now a man of property and doing well.

He took the steaming kettle from the trivet, and topped up dubious brandy with hot water, with which beverage they warmed themselves. After a while, Christopher, tongue loosened by spirits, found himself pouring out the full story of his Adelaide troubles.

'There ain't much doing for a fellow without capital,' said George, doubtfully, puffing on a cheap cigar and refilling their mugs. 'But you're welcome to stay here, on the house, until you find something. Of course, there's plenty of work out in the bush. The squatters are screaming out for labour now that transportation's finished. Chris, your father ain't badly off from what I've heard. Why don't you ask him to help you?'

'His heart's set on sheep. I don't like sheep. Never have. And I don't aim to take Laurie out into the bush. It isn't her sort of life.'

'I can see,' said George, who was becoming quite mellow, 'that I'll have to wean you from this tomfool notion of getting married. Life in front of you, old man. You don't want to waste it mooning over a girl five hundred miles away who'll turn into the worst shrew alive once she has that ring on her finger. Follow my example, Chris. Stay free. Plenty of girls without marriage lines.' He leaned forward and lowered his voice to a slurred whisper. 'Take Clara, my barmaid. All home comforts without the responsibility.'

Christopher had seen Clara, a full-busted brunette who wore too much rouge, and thought that she demonstrated George's poor taste.

'Until their fathers catch up with you,' he retorted, his tone edged by the memories of harsh experience.

'Plenty of girls without fathers,' replied George, smugly, and then held up a placating hand as his friend looked fit to explode. 'Listen to me. You know I went over to Captain Allard's place near Liverpool when he bought out Mr Watts? Same arrangement again. Living in the house with the family. Got so I couldn't stand another day of it. Captain Allard was a happy bachelor until he was forty-two. Then he got it into his head he needed heirs, so he married this pretty little widow. Belgian or something, she was. People went to England during the wars, and she married a fellow who got sent out with the New South Wales Corps, same as Captain Allard. Sweet as sugar until the knot was tied. Then it started. I'm telling you, she could strip the hide off him with her tongue without ever raising her voice. Never a naughty word. Oh no, she wasn't the vulgar sort. Flogger they used to call him in the old days. Tie a man to the iron triangle and then stand by and watch the blood spurt for the fun of it. Well, she paid him back in full. Every so often, about once a week, he'd get good and drunk, and weep into his glass, and tell me how he'd been so happy until that woman got her claws into him. Then there'd be a row because he had gotten drunk, and one night things got to such a pitch she tried to do away with herself. Slashed her wrists. Now, that was enough. I was gone as soon as I settled up to buy those sheep. Three days.'

Christopher stretched out his legs rather dreamily, and digested the other's tale.

'Did Captain Allard ever say anything about owing my father a favour?' he asked.

'A favour? To your father?' George stood up, not very steadily. 'Bit out of the Captain's orbit, I'd say. Now I'd better go and play mine host for a while. Just make yourself at home.'

Waking late the next day, with a shocking headache and a heaving stomach, Christopher decided that the last thing he would do in future was make himself at home on George's premises. Snatches of memory concerning Clara and another young woman made him shudder. George was definitely no fit companion for a steady young man who was unofficially engaged and had his way to make.

Therefore, he made it his immediate business to find accommodation in a cheap but decent boarding-house, and looked for a job. What was forthcoming was not very grand, and involved driving a dray for a tallow manufacturer.

There being a limit to the amount of mutton this small population could consume, even if meat featured on the menu three times a day, the pastoralists sold off their useless beasts to be boiled down for tallow. It was a noisome business, and already there were complaints above the sickly smells hovering over Melbourne and the amount of effluvium being poured into the Yarra Yarra from the factories, but the industry was profitable. Christopher managed to conquer his distaste for the unpleasant odours surrounding the factory, for the wages were reasonable, and Mr Ross, his employer, soon realised that young Kershaw was honest and hardworking.

As the months passed, he also discovered that Christopher, in addition to being strong and reliable, had a shrewd knowledge of stock and what it should cost. He was city bred himself, and until now had relied upon an agent to do his buying at the slaughteryards, but by sending his smart young employee instead, he saved himself money. Christopher was surprised at this: he had had no formal tuition in figures, but now, face to face with commercial problems for the first time in his life, he found that he had a quick and sure head for financial transactions.

Now his letters to Laurie were of an increasingly optimistic kind. He hoped soon, he wrote, to buy a block of land in a better part of town, and once that had happened, the day would not be far distant when he could think of building a house. Actually, he was indulging in a little daydreaming here. He was by no means well off. He lived quietly enough, but now that he had graduated from heaving barrels of tallow to bargaining at the stock sales, he needed city clothes.

He avoided the drinking and card parties which were the chief hobby of young bucks in a town where males far outnumbered females, and took lessons to improve his syntax from a rather mysterious, scholarly man of good background. For recreation, and to add weight to his arguments with the rougher characters he met in the course of business, he sparred in the boxing saloon next to George Forster's inn. Always in his mind was the thought that perhaps one day he would meet Stephen Allard again, and this time, he was determined, there would be no humiliating defeat.

When he wrote home to Bathurst, he could be excused for seeming a little smug. He was managing very nicely on his own, with a goal in sight, and everything set for prosperity and happiness. There were one or two minor worries, which he did not mention.

Mr Ross had an only daughter, Adelaide, named for King William's consort and not the town, which, of course, had not been in existence at the time of her birth. She was a fresh-faced, healthy girl of seventeen, and when Christopher was invited to Sunday dinner at his employer's home, he would have been quite stupid not to have realised that the girl was looking at him in a certain way. He liked her, in a detached, friendly fashion, but more and more he noticed that Mrs Ross made remarks which could only be construed as taking a lot for granted.

He did not wish to offend Mr Ross, but neither did he wish to become entangled with Adelaide, and he tried to make it clear, without hurting any feelings, that his interests lay elsewhere.

At the same time, he badly wanted Laurie at his side. Week by week, he counted his small savings, and tried to work out whether he could possibly afford to send her the fare necessary for the voyage to Melbourne. She was still under age, but he suspected that once she had left home, her parents would be relieved to have her respectably married, even to someone as undesirable as himself. She was no heiress being inveigled into matrimony by an adventurer, and he was no longer a stablehand, but a steady young man of business. On these grounds alone, he felt that, if necessary, he could apply to a magistrate for special permission to wed Laurel Fenwick.

Always at the back of his mind was the lurking fear that if he did not act quickly, Laurie would find a husband closer to home. The solution to the problem was money, sufficient to pay her fare from Adelaide with enough over to set up modest housekeeping.

The older Christopher Kershaw looked back at this besotted and desperate young man with some contempt. In his state of mind, he had been a sitting duck.

7

On principle, without being unfriendly about it, Kershaw had ben avoiding George Forster. He did not dislike George, but felt it wise not to pursue the friendship.

Sometimes, when he was engaged in a sparring bout at Sam Nesbitt's boxing saloon, George would come in from his premises next door, and watch for a while, and they usually exchanged a few words afterwards. The last time he had spoken to the publican, George had been hurt and downcast because Clara had suddenly decided to marry a young Scots immigrant.

'He's starting up farming,' George had explained, baffled as to why his paramour preferred hard times and a wedding ring to a soft life and keeping his bed warm. 'Nothing ahead of the silly chit but pinching and scraping and hard work.'

'They might do well,' remarked Christopher. 'You know how it is. Most land is under depasturage, and we have to import a lot of food.'

'It's not your girl who's going off to grow turnips,' snapped George.

Although Christopher felt that it served George right, it reminded him again that young women changed their minds . . . and thought a lot of the status attached to being married. Thus, when, a fortnight later, George placed a technically illegal proposition before him, he was in a frame of mind to accept.

'Chris,' said George, 'how would you like to earn twenty guineas?'

Christopher would have liked very much to earn twenty guineas, but he knew George well enough to be wary.

'I'll listen,' he said, offhandedly.

George explained.

Tomorrow week, that was the following Sunday, a prize-fight had been arranged to take place in a secret spot near Brighton, a village about six miles down the bay from Melbourne. A Cornishman, fresh out from triumphs in the Old Dart, was to have fought the Van Diemen's Land champion, one Derwent Dan O'Harrily, but this damn-fool Cornishman had got himself married to the servant girl at his lodgings, who had come out from his home county. This wretched woman, so sweet and loving, like all women before marriage, had, as soon as the band was firmly on her finger, denounced prizefighting and convinced the bloody fool that the only decent life for a Cornishman was with a pick and a lamp at the bottom of a hole. The result was that the Newlyn Fancy had renounced the boxing ring and gone off to South Australia to join all the other hymn-singing Cousin Jacks in the copper mines.

Now, Derwent Dan had arrived in Melbourne and found himself minus an opponent for the big bout. What made it worse, boxing enthusiasts from as far out as Geelong in one direction and Westernport Bay in the other were coming to see the renowned Van Diemonian. As he, George, had arranged all this, his reputation would suffer, and in addition, he would still have to pay off Dan.

'No,' said Christopher, 'not on your life.'

'Twenty guineas, just for appearing, Chris, and seventy-five's the purse if you win.'

'Go to hell,' jeered Christopher. 'Have all my teeth knocked out more likely.'

'You could give him a run for his money, lad,' said Sam Nesbitt, soothingly. 'And twenty guineas for no worse than you get here sometimes on Saturday night isn't to be sneezed at.'

'No,' answered Christopher, firmly, but the thought of that twenty guineas tantalized him. He refused George's offer, of course, but on Monday evening he dropped into the bar of

The Trafalgar Inn, and sensing that Forster was becoming desperate, hinted that if the fee were slightly raised, he might consider it.

Sunday morning was crisp and clear, and while the sun was still but a golden smear on the eastern horizon he was called for at his lodgings, to be transported in a gig over bumpy tracks to a cleared paddock near the village of Brighton. The bout was scheduled for nine in the morning, and by the time he arrived, a large crowd was already gathering to enjoy the forbidden spectacle.

However, as young Kershaw peered out from his tent, he felt a deep qualm which was not due to the prospect of being pounded silly by Derwent Dan. Many of those present, irrespective of social standing, were wearing either green or orange rosettes.

Derwent Dan, judging by his surname, was the champion of those wearing green rosettes, for Irishmen had brought with them across the oceans all their conflicting loyalties for two monarchs long dead, to wit, King William and King James. Christopher had learnt a little about English history from books borrowed from the Mechanics' Institute, but he was blowed if he could see why Irishmen became so worked up over two men who had been in their graves for about a century and a half. He thought that Queen Victoria was a nice young lady, and he was content to leave his interest in royalty at that.

It needed no great deductive skill to realise that he was going to be champion of those adherents to the Orange cause, and he did not like it at all. Win or lose, he was going to find himself unpopular with some of Melbourne's large Irish population. Then, as so often happens, he found that he had been considering things from the wrong angle. As he and his opponent went out to face each other, a man he had never seen before began an exhortation.

'On our left, gentlemen, we have

the Van Diemen's Land champion, Derwent Dan O'Harrily, undefeated in two years.'

Christopher had already sized up Derwent Dan as the nastiest specimen he had ever seen. Dan was about his own age, and matched him in weight and size, but whereas he considered himself a clean-cut specimen of New South Wales manhood, this evil fellow from across the Bass Straits looked as if he had been born and raised within the sinister confines of the notorious Model Prison down at Port Arthur.

A mighty cheer went up, not from the wearers of the green as Christopher had expected, but from King William's supporters, while the adherents of King James booed and screamed and called Derwent Dan an assortment of insulting names. Out of the corner of his eye, Kershaw saw something which made him even gloomier. On the outskirts of the crowd, bets were being laid and money was changing hands at a great rate.

'On our right, Kit Kelly, the Currency Lad from Bathurst!'

All the green rosettes cheered, and someone yelled out that he remembered Kit's old Da in Cork years ago. In the background, Christopher saw George Forster grinning from ear to ear, and he knew that he had been painted in a very false colour, green to be exact. Laurie, Laurie, he thought wildly, suppressing his urge to bolt, always remember that I did this for you!

Before he could think any more, the bell was rung, and he found himself fighting the first — and last — prizefight of his life. During the first two premier rounds, they sparred cautiously, landing a jab here and there, but in the main prancing about and sizing each other up, while the crowd grew noisier and urged them to draw blood. Christopher began to feel more confident, for during the next round he had cause to wonder how Derwent Dan had won his reputation. Several punches which looked strong enough to fell an ox barely brushed his skin. In the sixth round, they joined, and as Derwent Dan lightly pummelled his ribs, before the referee separated them, Christopher heard him say, softly but clearly, 'Knock me out in the eighth round.'

Kershaw thought that he had been imagining things, and in fact, in the eighth he took a lot of punishment, but during the ninth, close in again, Derwent Dan hissed into his ear.

'Knock me out, yer bloody fool!'

Christopher knocked him out, and Derwent Dan fell to the earth convincingly unconscious, and the referee counted to ten. The crowd went berserk, and someone began singing a song about the Siege of Londonderry in a fine Irish tenor, which was fortunate, because members of the green faction were rushing in to chair the victor, and Christopher was too appalled at the turn of event to wish to accept acclaim.

Within a minute, orange and green

were at it hammer and tongs, and in the confusion, the beaver hats of the 'gentry' were knocked to the ground, resulting in a scrimmage which drew in nearly everyone present. Derwent Dan revived very suddenly and grinned at Christopher as he towelled away the water which had been tossed over him by his second. Shaking the victor by the hand, he said that Christopher had put on a good show and that he hoped for a return bout before too long.

At that moment, someone yelled that the constables were coming, and Christopher, seeing George Forster's big chestnut gelding tethered nearby, leapt on to the animal's saddle, and, still wearing his tights, headed towards Melbourne at a gallop.

Of course, he told George exactly what he thought of him, and after a few seconds' tightlipped silence, George produced a small bag and plonked it down on Christopher's bed, for Forster had sought out his bruised and weary friend at his lodgings.

'There's your money.'

'Keep it.'

'Don't be a damned fool. You earned it.'

Christopher picked up the bag with the intention of heaving it at George's head, but the other was too quick, and was out of the room with the door shut behind him before he could take aim. The bag was heavier than he had expected, and the coins jingled temptingly. He sighed, loosened the string, and tipped the contents out on to the grey blanket which covered his bed in spartan style.

The wages of sin, he thought, and began to count. It came to ninety-eight pounds and two shillings, made up of the twenty-two guineas he had demanded for appearing, and the seventy-five pounds due to him as victor.

What could he do?

He decided to send sufficient to Laurie to pay her fare to Melbourne, and invest the rest in a block of land.

The next morning, Mr Ross called him into his office and told him that he was sorry, but he would have to finish up at the end of the week. For himself, he did not care what Christopher did in his spare time, but his wife had strong views about Sunday observance, and strong ideas about Roman Catholics, and that was that. Christopher was no more a Roman Catholic than the Emperor of China, and he was astounded that news could travel so fast. He knew, however, that Mrs Ross was not a woman to brook argument, so that was the end of his good position with the tallow manufacturer.

Well, what of it? He'd go over to Adelaide and talk Laurie into eloping with him. He had enough money to tide them over for a while, until he settled into something else.

8

On the same day as he received Laurie's letter, there was also one from Miss Sophia Fenwick. Miss Sophia implored him not to think too badly of her niece. There were circumstances, she wrote, which she could not explain out of family loyalty, but he must try to take this blow bravely, etc., etc.

He tore up that letter in disgust and flung it away before doing the same to Laurie's note.

'Dearest Kit,' it ran, 'By the time you receive this I shall be a married woman. Please try to forgive me, and do not write to me again.'

So, there it was, the end to what had after all been some extremely foolish dreams. The Fenwicks had hardly a penny, but they were gentry. Even if he had become rich instead of being an out-of-work common prizefighter, they would still turn up their noses at him.

As for those circumstances, so direly hinted at by Miss Sophia — well, if young Laurie had carried on with her habit of creeping out of a night into a man's arms, he could guess what they were. For a while, he pondered on trying to find out her husband's name and sending him those letters penned so recklessly by the Fenwicks' youngest daughter. Laurie had seemed shy on that night when the doctor had caught them, but when it came to writing letters, her goose quill flew across the paper and criss-crossed back again with a passionate fervour bordering on the madly indiscreet.

He decided that such a course was beneath him, and threw the letters into the fire. Then he went out and got himself thoroughly drunk.

When he sobered up the next day, he knew that he had left the old soft-headed, soft-hearted Christopher Kershaw behind him for ever. He was going to show them all, the Allards, the Fenwicks, the whole confounded lot of them, the snobs in the Melbourne Club, the arrogant young squatters who rode into town and made nuisances of themselves by racing their horses along the main streets, every man Jack of them.

One day he would be rich, and it would be his turn.

He had no means of knowing that even as he made this resolution, Laurie was walking to her wedding at Holy Trinity Church a few hundred yards along Adelaide's North Terrace. Good winds had sent her letter to her former sweetheart a little quicker than she had anticipated.

Her father held her arm, and behind her walked her still unmarried sister, Louisa, holding the best posy Adelaide's gardens could offer on this cloudy April day. Following the first autumn rains, the reserves on the other side of the road were green, and in the middle distance, red-coated soldiers drilled, watched by children and a few ragged aboriginals. Housewives came to their gates to see the modest wedding procession pass. There were those who tut-tutted and said that it was a shame.

Others thought that Miss Laurel Fenwick had done well for herself, considering the rumours one heard about the doctor's financial troubles. A fine doctor was Robert Fenwick, but a fool with money. *And* there had been whispers about Miss Laurel and a thoroughly unsuitable young man who had worked for a while at Nelson's Livery Stables. Not at all the thing for the Fenwicks.

It must have been like this going to the guillotine, thought Laurie, still clutching at romantic fancies to appease her bruised heart. Laurie never quite saw herself as a real person, rather as a character in a continuing drama. It was a common enough feminine failing, liable to land her in trouble at times, but at others offering a shield of sorts against life's unpleasant realities.

When her mother had first told her that Mr Harden had offered for her, she had laughed. She had known Mr Harden ever since they had arrived in South Australia. He and his second wife, dead since of pneumonia, had pitched their tent adjacent to that of the Fenwicks behind the sandhills at Holdfast Bay, where immigrants had endured several uncomfortable weeks before moving to their town lots in Adelaide, six miles inland. Together, the families had weathered extreme heat, mosquitoes, a fire which swept frighteningly close to the encampment, and violent thunderstorms during which they had to crouch under opened umbrellas within their saturated tents.

Mr Harden had flourished financially. He was a lawyer by profession, and naturally shrewd in money matters. While Dr Fenwick lost money in land speculation, Mr Harden accumulated it. Later, as the colony struggled to its feet, he had been singularly lucky in copper mining, whilst, as usual, Dr

Fenwick had lost heavily.

The irony was that they were rivals in the same mining venture. Copper had been discovered in great quantities in several areas north of Adelaide, and there being many Cornishmen amongst the South Australian settlers, men with mining knowledge were readily available. Following one such strike, two companies were formed in Adelaide, each claiming prior right to the new find. Litigation was the consequence, the two rival groups being nicknamed the Nobs and the Snobs. However, when news arrived that a Sydney syndicate had enough cash in hand to buy the twenty thousand acres of land under debate, the Nobs and Snobs temporarily pooled their resources. (The South Australian administration, unlike that in the eastern colonies, preferred to sell rather than lease land.) Cash being short in Adelaide at that time, the twenty thousand pounds required was a hard-won sum. Dr Fenwick, plunging heavily on behalf of the Nobs, and sure that at last fortune awaited him, borrowed deeply.

The land remained safely in South Australian hands, but time came for the division. A line was drawn across the middle, and a coin tossed to decide which party should have the first choice. The Snobs, for the most part comprising shopkeepers, tradesmen and small farmer — and Mr Harden — won the toss, and chose the northern section, the southern going to the more elite Nobs.

Typically, the Nobs called their portion The Princess Royal. The Snobs stuck by the native Burra Burra, and while the Princess Royal proved to be almost useless, Burra Burra made its investors a fortune.

Laurie had lived with her family's money troubles since childhood. They were a part of existence, and somehow the Fenwicks managed to live reasonably well and keep up appearances. This time, however, the end had really come. There were mysterious things called Bills and Notes which were falling due. No one actually said that Mr Harden was buying himself a young bride. He was prepared to make a settlement by taking up some of those Bills and Notes.

He doted on Laurie, said Mrs Fenwick, and he was a good man. There had never been a breath of scandal attached to his name, and there had been plenty of those sizzling through Adelaide's tiny, close-knit community in the first years. Quarrels, the Surveyor-General's common-law wife, and a real wife elsewhere who was a scandal in herself, hard drinkers, and many episodes which had been blown up out of all proportion.

Laurie stared out of the window determinedly.

'No,' she said.

'I hope,' said her mother, tartly, 'that you aren't still thinking about that dreadful young man from New South Wales. And to think that we

120

took him into our home! What a way to repay us, by trying to seduce our youngest daughter.'

'Mother, it was nothing of the sort. And Kit is not a dreadful young man.' Laurie kept her voice even, although inside her embarrassment and disgust rose again. Those letters to Christopher Kershaw had never hinted at her trials after Dr Fenwick had found them together.

Laurie and her mother were not close. Mrs Fenwick dutifully loved her children, but she did not really like Laurel. Perhaps it was because this child had proved to be her most difficult, and last, confinement, leaving her with impaired health. Or perhaps it was because the fair-haired girl, with her alternate moods of impetuosity and dreamy romanticism, reminded her too strongly of her sister-in-law, Sophia, and thus, of her own husband. Sophia, to Mrs Fenwick, was another burden to bear, a silly woman who had once tried to elope to America with, of all things, a gamekeeper.

When Laurel's duplicity was exposed, it was a clear case of history repeating itself. As well, it fell to Mrs Fenwick to discover how far the girl's folly had led her. Too inhibited to tackle the task herself, she handed it on to Jane, as her eldest daughter, Estelle, was too far away to help in this crisis.

Jane, unwilling, but armed with the knowledge of twelve months' married life and an impending confinement, went into the room once occupied by the convalescent Christopher, where Laurie had been practically a prisoner since that dreadful moment at the stables. Finally, after some dodging about with refined allusions and careful questions, Jane made her meaning clear to her red-eyed but unrepentant sister. Laurie, innocence finally stripped away, burst into fresh tears, but through the sobs she managed to state her feelings.

'I wish I had! Then I'd have to marry him!'

How futile this declaration seemed all those months later, as she felt the trap of marriage to Mr Harden fastening about her. For weeks, she had suspected that it was 'in the wind', while at the same time hoping that nothing would come of it. Now her mother spoke openly about the probability of a proposal.

'What a foolish girl you are! He'll never come back. He wouldn't dare. Your father made Adelaide too hot for him.'

'When I'm of age, I'm going to marry him!' She swung round, angry, discretion forgotten. 'We write, every week, and we'll go on writing.'

'How?' Mrs Fenwick's tone was ominous. 'No letters have come to this house. Do you mean to say that you've been conducting a clandestine correspondence behind our backs?'

When anger subsided, her mother came back to the hard fact of imminent impoverishment.

'Why can't he choose Louisa?'

demanded Laurie defiantly, but she knew the reason. Mr Harden wanted her. He made that increasingly clear by his glances, his smiles, and the kindly and charming way in which he addressed her.

The most distressing part was that she did not dislike Mr Harden. She wanted to hate him and could not. She was actually fond of him as one would be fond of a good and generous uncle. Neither was she unaware of the way in which her father had aged of late.

It was as if he knew that this was the last chance. He was no longer young, and quite unable to start again. He was not a dishonest man, and had he been of a more stable nature financially, he would have by now been in a prosperous way. His old friend James Harden was well off, and although Dr Fenwick believed that some of the capital had come to him through his first wife, and was actually entailed to their two sons, who lived in England, the desperate man saw, besides relief from his own troubles, a comfortable future for a daughter with something of his own weaknesses in her makeup.

He was furiously angry when he learned that Laurie had corresponded for over a year with that unspeakable young upstart. Further probing revealed that his sister Sophia had been the instigator. That was Sophia all over, hopelessly irresponsible, and trying to live her life second hand.

While tantrums and rages flew about the household, Laurie came to grips with the unpalatable truth, and being Laurie, she managed to make it acceptable. She was going to sacrifice herself for the others. This attitude took her through the worst weeks of her young life. She brought out all her dearest Kit's letters from their hiding place, and wept as she re-read them before casting them into the fire. She hoped, bravely, that he would find another love, and at the same time prayed that he would never forget her.

She did falter at the door of the

church when she saw James Harden standing before the altar rail, elegant, distinguished, but indubitably middle-aged.

When Laurie awoke the next morning, it took some moments before she realised where she was. This big room with the long windows was so different from the small chamber she shared with Louisa, with its outlook of other people's back yards. She turned, and saw Mr Harden lying beside her, and then, for the first time during the past twenty-four hours, she had to fight to keep back tears. His nightcap had fallen off, and his hair was grey. Grey!

Her movement awakened him, and he reached for her young body, caressing so expertly that, almost against her will, she was aroused. But, even as they made love, her mind was registering the colour of the canopy above the bed.

How hideous, she thought. That ugly puce shade must have been chosen by his last wife, poor Aunt Emily. I shall change it as soon as possible.

Her mind began working busily on colour schemes and fabrics. Laurie had discovered that the way to survival was through an obsession with trivialities.

9

On a fine Sunday afternoon the following October, Christopher passed the time strolling about the streets of Melbourne. He had spent the winter travelling north to Bathurst and back again, for having invested his ill-gotten prizefight money in a block of land, he now thought of Melbourne as his base. The journey home had taught him that he had been away too long. He loved his parents dearly, and thought that his sister Joanna was growing into the prettiest girl ever born, but their ways were no longer his ways.

He had hoped for a confrontation with the Allards, but Mrs Allard had died just before his arrival, and Stephen and Percy had crossed the ranges to be with the rest of the family. There was some talk in Bathurst that it was a shame, as the youngest child and only girl was the same age as his sister, the age, said the wiseheads, when a girl needed her mother, and that old rip Captain Allard was no substitute for maternal care.

Christopher thought that it all served them right, and that anything which upset the lives of people like the Allards — and the Fenwicks — was on his side.

Today, it seemed, everyone was out taking advantage of the warm and fine conditions, a wise precaution in this town where a pleasant day too often presaged gales, rainstorms, fogs, frosts, duststorms, or sticky, fly-ridden humidity, according to the season.

On a vacant allotment in Great Bourke Street, one of the east-west streets, a meeting was in progress, and as Kershaw neared the spot he could see that the banner held aloft behind the platform advertised this as a total abstinence rally.

He stood on the outskirts of the crowd, listening to the woman who spoke from the platform. She was well known in Melbourne, and her devotion to the cause was all the more remarkable because she had arrived in Port Phillip on board a ship, captained by her own husband, which carried a cargo of spirits. Although denounced by those who declared it against Holy Writ for a woman to speak from a public platform, and ridiculed by the publicans, Mrs Dalgarno had a large following.

Kershaw only half-listened, for his eye had been caught by the smiling glance of a fresh-faced, willowy girl who stood a few yards away in the company of a young married couple he knew by sight. It was Adelaide Ross, and he returned her smile with a formal nod, deliberately ignoring the inviting little toss of her head, so demurely covered by her fashionable bonnet. Her very name, Adelaide, stirred the other hurt he was endeavouring to forget, and his pride still rankled over the way in which her mother had judged and condemned him without a full knowledge of the facts.

All right. He had been a fool to let George talk him into fighting Derwent Dan, but since he had returned to Melbourne three days ago, he had discovered that most persons present on that bright April morning treated the affair as a huge joke.

'Ha ha, me foine Oirish boyo!' accompanied by a hearty slap on the back was a greeting he had endured several times from persons who each thought that they were being very original and witty.

He thought, if Adelaide comes over here I'll talk to her nicely, but I've had enough of women and their ways for a bit. I'm certainly not going out of my way to renew the friendship, if it ever was that.

After three minutes more, Kershaw decided to move on in search of more congenial entertainment, but just then Mrs Dalgarno introduced the next speaker, who, she declared, would tell the audience all the scarifying details of his rescue from the pits of alcoholic degradation. There was applause, and a lanky, very lined fellow in his fifties hopped up on to the platform and grinned a lopsided, gap-toothed grin at the assembly.

He was not an educated man, but what he lacked in refinement and syntax was amply replaced by a racy style which held his listeners, none more so than Christopher Kershaw, in a state of fascination.

He went into details of his childhood's horrors, relating how, after the demise of his drunken mother, he had been left in the care of a stepfather who had been murdered during a drinking party with some blacks. This led in turn to his adoption by a poor, ignorant black woman, who had taken him into her tribe, and cared for him lovingly, until she too had fallen prey to liquor.

'I saw 'er out at Parramatta, just before she died,' he said, staring about the upturned, enthralled faces, and wiping away a tear. 'The poor, wild thing was skin and bones, and even while she was coughin' out her very 'eart, she still 'eld out her 'and, beggin' for money to buy drink! If she'd been an 'orse, good people, I'd 'ave shot 'er to put 'er out of 'er misery.'

Tumultuous applause greeted this, for as drunken aboriginals were a pitifully common sight in Melbourne streets, it hit right home.

This was only the beginning. Now the orator told them how, even with such hideous examples before him all his days, he had himself yielded to temptation and taken to the easy release of rum. At this point, he paused to give the moment its full drama, for a second wavering as he saw Christopher at the back of the crowd, but almost immediately he recovered himself and continued.

'You ever seen a bunyip?' he demanded. 'You ain't? Pray to heaven you don't, good people. It's so 'orrible I can't describe it with ladies present,

but let me tell you, bunyips are nothin'
to what you see when youse got the
'orrors!'

Christopher laughed, and was hushed
and glared at until he composed himself
to hear the rest.

'I tell you, ladies and gentlemen,
the great black pit yawned in front o'
me, writhin' and seethin' with things
so awful I nearly faints just to think
of 'em. Somehow, I pulled meself
together and staggered, no, that's a lie,
I crawled — *crawled* on me 'ands and
knees — out of the stinkin' stable back
of that public-house, and got to the
water butt and drank that wonderful,
pure, clean water until the 'orrors was
washed away. And from that day to
this, I ain't ever touched another drop
of strong drink!'

Clapping thundered across the calm,
warm afternoon, scaring off a few
cockatoos which had perched on a
gum tree nearby, and Mrs Dalgarno's
thanks for this (she said) unsolicited
testimonial could barely be heard.

'Good to see you, Young Cornstalk,' declared Hughie Deane, pumping the younger man's hand up and down. 'And seein' the light, I hope?'

'It's good to see you, Old Cornstalk. What are you doing here in Melbourne?'

'Well, Chris, I got thrown from my horse a while back. Since then, I've been living soft 'ere in town. Funny I hadn't run into you before, but I drive a dray and I'm out of town a bit.'

The younger man explained that he had been up north to Bathurst, and had returned on the previous Thursday. Then:

'Is all that stuff you were spouting back there true?'

Hughie Deane laughed, his face folding into deep creases.

'Y'know how it is. You got to dress things up a bit so people'll listen. It's true in parts, anyhow. Now, what are you going to do now you're back?'

Christopher admitted that he would have to find work, probably out in the bush, as there did not seem to be much doing in town, with so many unemployed immigrants looking for work.

'I'm throwin' up my job,' announced the other. 'Goin' back drovin'. Can't stand this bein' closed in.'

The two men had reached an intersection, and to their south, beyond the spars of a ship lying in the Yarra Yarra, the green knoll called Emerald Hill rose beyond the swamps on the far bank of the river. To their west, waterfowl circled above the swamps. Northwards, past the sheep and horses grazing on town lots, was Flagstaff Hill, where the ball was raised each day at noon to keep Melbourne's clocks in order, and the tall flagpole stood bare, for this afternoon no ship from Britain had been sighted beating up the bay with a precious cargo of news from Home. To the east, forest formed a screen beyond the town's limit.

'Tell you what,' continued Deane. 'Why don't you try for my job?'

This, then, was how Christopher

came to work for Mr Greaves. If he had known where it would lead, thought the older Kershaw, watching the first of an angry dawn lighting a sky stained with dust, he would have gone droving with Hughie Deane. There was not much future in droving, but not much distress, either.

Before Hughie Deane left, Christopher apologised to the other for not being able to return the money paid to Dr Fenwick. Old Cornstalk seemed taken aback.

'Lor, lad, that was never a debt. It was a gift.' He grinned, slyly. 'I ain't gettin' any younger. Some day I'll need a helping hand. Save it until then.'

Mr Greaves had a store at the western end of town, handy to the landing place on the river, but he did not bother much about selling to the general public, as his interest lay in the direct supply of goods to farmers and pastoralists. He was also a haulage contractor, and in a fairly prosperous way of business. He had a well-built two-storeyed stone house of about eight rooms separated from his store by a vacant block where he kept his drays. Actually, most of the business was handled by his son of a former marriage, for Mr Greaves did not enjoy good health, and Christopher soon learnt by hearsay and observation that young Mr Greaves and his wife did not get along with the other Mrs Greaves.

Kershaw, having found out just how important it was to keep in favour with his employer's wife, was always as polite as possible to Mrs Greaves the elder, although she was a person to whom he had taken an instant dislike. She was small and auburn-haired, and although well into her thirties, her complexion was smooth and her figure youthful in its suppleness. She looked down on everyone working for her husband, and called Christopher 'My man' or 'You there' in accents which sounded as if she had the proverbial plum in her mouth. Her life, he understood, was devoted to social climbing and being accepted into the better class of Melbourne people, who were inclined to despise 'trade'.

Shortly before the end of that first year, which was the time when things improved for him, he had a surprise encounter with Clara, George Forster's former mistress.

She was now Mrs Gilmore, and judging by the infant in a crib and the state of her figure, had settled down to populating the country with all speed. As Christopher, in charge of a dray-load of supplies for her husband, arrived outside the gate in front of the small timber and bark-roofed cottage, she looked extremely wary.

'Why, it's Mr Kershaw, isn't it?' she said, sending him urgent messages with her eyes.

'Yes, that's right. And . . . ?' He was surprised to meet her here in this pleasant valley about twenty miles north of Melbourne, but, with her husband at his side, he had the quickness of wit to ask to be reminded whom she might be.

'I was Clara Hayes.'

'Yes, I remember. Nice place you've got here.'

She smiled, in appreciation of his tact, while her husband looked pleased at the compliment to his industry. The visitor wondered just how much Gilmore had known about Clara's way of life. Not that one could blame poor Clara. She had been one of those luckless girl immigrants dumped on the Sydney wharves back in the days before the authorities had been prodded into making proper provision for their arrival in New South Wales. One could only guess at the seamy little adventures which had preceded her association with George Forster, who, to do him justice, had treated her kindly and generously.

Driving away, Christopher decided that Clara had landed on her feet, and good luck to her — and to the husband who had recognised the decent woman underneath Clara's flashy exterior. Now that he had met Edward Gilmore, he appreciated Clara's perspicacity in preferring the Scotsman to George. He was a hardworking man, who in addition to slaving day after day clearing land and raising the crops Melbourne needed so badly in this country where agriculture took second place to sheep and cattle, had still found time to erect a brush fence about the cottage, to afford protection from winds and keep out straying stock. It reminded Christopher of his own father, who, he recalled, had spent precious hours many years ago, when he himself was still a child, to dig over a patch of ground in front of the shack so that his mother could grow some of the flowers she so loved.

He still saw the picture in his mind, of Pa with his arm about Ma's shoulders, as the pair of them stood and admired that little patch of broken soil. They had still been desperately poor at the time, but a garden bed was a gift beyond price to Molly Kershaw.

Yes, Clara had chosen wisely. Perhaps she had to work very hard, and would bear too many children, but she had a fine man at her side.

For Kershaw, it was to be the story of his job with Mr Ross all over again, without the unfortunate ending. Unlike most of the men who took the bullock-drawn drays along the unspeakably bad bush tracks to outlying homesteads, he was shrewd and full of initiative, prompted by an ambition to prove that he was an equal to people like the Allards and the Fenwicks. Promoted to assisting young Mr Greaves, he took his city clothes out of their mothballs, and watched out for every opportunity to make himself indispensable.

Unhappily, now that he had been elevated, he found himself in the front row as an audience to the drama being played out within the Greaves family circle. The summer that year was very humid, with days when the sunlight wavered with the moisture in the air, and the frequent thunderstorms brought only passing relief, for as soon as the clouds had gone, the evaporation increased the discomfort. This irritating and tiring weather added to the tensions between Mrs Greaves and her stepson and his wife. Never a day passed without young Mrs Greaves running out to her husband in tears, or old Mr Greaves coming to his son and asking, awkwardly and shyly, that he apologise to his stepmother 'for the sake of my grandchildren'. It was hardly a shock when the son, his young wife, and the two children, packed up suddenly after what must have been a quite irrevocable disagreement, and took ship for South Africa, where young Mrs Greaves had relatives.

'That woman,' young Mr Greaves told Christopher as they shook hands in farewell, 'is a fiend straight out of Hell. Take my advice and keep out of her way.'

Old Mr Greaves looked very upset

for weeks, but Kershaw sensed that here was opportunity, and determined that the business would not suffer from Mr Greaves' neglect while the dust settled from the explosion, he quietly took over the management. He did not push himself forward, nor ask for more money, because he thought he had judged Mr Greaves rightly, and sure enough, after about two months, Mr Greaves had a private talk with him and, unexpectedly, offered him a third share in the business.

The young man was thunderstruck. He had expected higher wages, but not this, and he mumbled that he could not accept it. In the end, Mr Greaves took the hundred pounds Christopher had saved so painfully, documents were drawn up, and everything was duly signed and sealed.

'I'm not such a fool as you might think,' said Mr Greaves as they both sipped sherry after the agreement had been signed. 'You're a hard worker, and you're smart, and you're under an obligation to me, and while I have two-thirds, you'll do as I say.'

Thus, although he was better off materially, Christopher was in bondage to Mr Greaves, but with his third share of the profits, plus his salary, he was not inclined to grumble.

10

'I've heard you've had a bit of good luck,' said George Forster, with a decided leer. 'Virtue's its own reward, or something, eh?'

Christopher had long avoided George Forster, but they had met face to face on the footpath a short distance along the street from the Greaves' stores. He had nodded, and intended to pass, but the other reached out and gripped his arm, so that there was no escape short of an undignified tussle.

'I've worked hard enough,' he countered. 'I'm in a hurry, George, so you'll have to excuse me.'

It was a fib on a Sunday afternoon, but any other day of the week it would have been absolutely true, for he was always in a hurry on working days, kept constantly on the run by the demands of a flourishing business. He had now come to recognise that respectability was a decided commercial asset, and did not particularly wish to be seen standing in the street talking with rakish George Forster, publican and fight fixer.

'Look', said George, almost angrily, 'I know what you've been thinking for the past two years, and you had no right to think it about an old friend. Damn it, Chris, what sort of fool do you take me for? I've a position in this town. Standing for alderman next council elections. Admit I like a bit of fun, but my family has standing in Sydney these days. Can't let them down. I can make money without becoming a criminal. Put you up in good faith, and paid you what I promised to pay you. Didn't know Derwent Dan was tied up with the bookmakers, and that's my word on it.'

Christopher said nothing, not entirely convinced, and yet wanting at the same time to believe his old friend.

'And if you don't believe me, you

ain't so bloody Simon Pure yourself, you know!'

With this outburst, George, whose even temper was a byword, turned to stalk away.

'All right, George. Let's consider it all past.'

They shook hands, and George explained why he was in the neighbourhood.

'I was looking for you,' he said, as they walked back towards George's new hotel, a solid building set back a little from the street, with a gravelled yard in front to allow patrons to be driven right to the very door. This was no low tavern catering for sailors or bush workers in town to drink up their wages. It was a substantial inn catering for a better-class clientele, a place where a man could lodge himself and his family, and be assured of clean, decent surroundings.

'Yes?'

'What about joining the Anti-Transportation League, old chap?'

By this time, they were settled in George's private parlour, but nowadays there was no cheap brandy and hot water, but tea and cakes served by a prim housekeeper in tidy grey covered by a spotless starched white apron.

'What a fool I'd look,' said Christopher when the servant had left. 'Me, with Pa and Ma both transported.'

'All part of the past. The present is what we're worried about. You know some of the squatters are trying to bring back transportation here in New South Wales? Bad enough having it still in Van Diemen's Land — all that trash sneaking over here and making damned nuisances of themselves. But if you're a big squatter, you don't have to pay a convict, or provide a decent house for him to live in.'

With this, he produced a poster from a drawer, and thrust it across to Christopher. The contents, in big black type, advised those citizens of Melbourne who had a vote in the forthcoming municipal elections that

Geo. Bailey Forster intended standing for the post of alderman in his ward. Mr Forster was a prominent member of the Anti-Transportation League, and very active in support of separation of the Port Phillip District from New South Wales. If elected, he intended to press for better street lighting in Melbourne, surfacing of town roads, the strict policing of building regulations, and an improvement in the water supply. Mr Forster, well known for the orderly way in which his public-houses had been conducted, had been a resident of Melbourne for five years, and was fully aware of the many problems faced by the growing town.

Well, I'll be damned, thought Christopher. What's come over him? Anti-Transportation League! The damned hypocrite wouldn't be here, any more than I would be, if it wasn't for transportation.

What had come over George was that metamorphosis which often overtakes those who find themselves becoming well-to-do men of property. From being a wild young buck, living only for the day, he was fast changing into a solid citizen with an eye on the future protection of his own interests. He also happened to be genuinely public-spirited.

Until now, Christopher had been too involved with his own problems to give much attention to the stories that certain powerful men in New South Wales were lobbying in London to have transportation to the eastern mainland resumed. But, having had the matter drawn to his attention, he knew that he was right behind George.

George thereupon gave him a bundle of posters to distribute and sold him a ticket to a social evening the following week, the purpose being to raise funds for the League, to offset printing costs and other expenses. So it was that Christopher met Adelaide Ross again, for her father was actively behind the League, and although he was conscious of disapproving glares from Mrs Ross, who had never forgiven him over the prizefight episode, they engaged in pleasant conversation and stood up for two dances together.

Mrs Ross, he gathered, had her eye on George for her attractive daughter. He wondered just how much Mrs Ross really knew about George.

As weeks passed he found himself thinking of Adelaide in terms of when they were married. She was comfortable to be with, and she accepted him as he was. However, he wanted more out of a relationship with a woman than Adelaide could offer. He wanted to feel as he had felt about Laurie, mad to hold her, to protect her, to tell the whole world to go to hell for her. Yet, where had that got him? Licking his wounds and nursing bitter feelings!

Summer eased into autumn, and other events occurred to take his mind off both the League and Adelaide Ross. Mr Greaves suffered a mild stroke during April, and the whole responsibility for the business fell upon young Kershaw. For convenience, he shifted goods from the smaller storeroom at the store, and turned it into rough living quarters for himself. By the time he put in a bed and a chair, and a few hooks for his clothes, there was not much room for anything else. The arrangement meant that he was right on the premises at opening time, and as the bullock-drawn vehicles left at dawn for their long journeys out into the bush, this was necessary, and allowed him a few extra minutes in bed. He took his meals at a place in the next street, and as he himself sometimes rode out of town for two or three days, this was not only more convenient than taking full board and lodging, but saved him money as well.

Mrs Greaves invited him to share their own table, but he managed to excuse himself. He liked Mr Greaves, but with her husband recovering his health in bed, he would have to eat alone with Mrs Greaves, and he still could not stand her, with her superior up-and-down glances and her constant name-dropping. She reminded him very much of Laurie's sister Louisa, who, having been born the beauty of the family, considered that the world owed her everything. Perhaps that is why she married Mr Greaves. Too particular about her suitors, and too wrapped up in her own attributes, she had let years slide by until she was glad to accept a bluff North Country widower.

Maggie Ryan, Mrs Greaves' maid-servant, was another enigma, for she was as much Hindu as Irish. Christopher marvelled that Mr Greaves had been able to stand both Mrs Greaves and that dark, exotic woman who glided round their house in a mysterious fashion and had the disconcerting habit of suddenly appearing from shadowy places as if she were forever sneaking about and eavesdropping.

Mr Greaves was up and about again in June, with the aid of a walking-stick, although he appeared quite feeble and old compared with the hearty, solid man he had been. He was cheerful, and went through the accounts with Kershaw, expressing satisfaction at the way in which things were going. Later, despite the other's warnings that he must not tire himself, he sat down and wrote several letters in his careful, round hand.

Watching him, his junior partner wondered again why Mr Greaves had chosen to start a new life in Melbourne. He was much older than the usual settler, and Christopher had gathered that he had income other than that from the business and could have easily retired upon the gains of his earlier labours. Mrs Greaves fluttered in then, and told her husband that he must not exert himself so, and she put her arms about his shoulders and looked at the younger man over his head, as if blaming him. Her gaze was so penetrating that he felt uncomfortable, and excused himself to go outside and check up on a team which had just returned.

He was asking the teamster about the state of the bullocks after a long haul on very bad roads when Mrs Greaves ran out from the office.

'Mr Kershaw, quickly!' Her usual superior manner had vanished, and her face was white with fright. He ran inside, and saw Mr Greaves lying on the floor, one foot still twisted in a rung of the chair upon which he had been seated. It was obvious that he had suffered another stroke.

'Now you send for the doctor, Mrs Greaves,' ordered Christopher. 'Ben here'll help me carry him to the house.'

But Mrs Greaves fell on her knees beside her husband, moaning and weeping, so that the young man had to lift her to her feet, whereupon she pressed her face against his shoulder, and he had to disengage himself very quickly, for her neat body had fitted against his in a way which at any other time he would have found astonishing.

'Please take hold of yourself. He's

alive, but you must send for the doctor.'

For one moment, he thought that she was going to fling herself against him again, but her eyes, which for an instant had been wide open and staring into his, half-closed again, and then, dabbing at her cheeks with a scrap of lace-edged lawn, she ran off to do his bidding.

This time, there was little hope that Mr Greaves would ever leave his bed again. He was paralysed down his right side, and after about a month he managed to talk in a blurred, painful fashion.

One day, Kershaw was visiting. He read part of the newspaper out to Mr Greaves, and then, quite out of the blue, the sick man said, 'I want you to buy me out, Chris.'

'Buy you out, sir?'

'Yes.' Every word Mr Greaves uttered was an effort, but now he motioned the other to bend low over the bed so that he would not have to speak loudly. 'You could, Chris. You've a third share now, and you're careful with your brass. You could borrow the rest from a bank. I won't be running things again.'

'I'd have to go pretty deep into debt, Mr Greaves,' he demurred. 'Why do you want me to take over?'

'I built it up from nowt, lad, and I don't care to see it go back to nowt. You know the ropes.'

He lay silent for a little while, recovering his strength, while Christopher stared out of the window, not really seeing the lowering mist which was once again dimming out the sunlight.

'I want to buy my wife an annuity. Think about it, lad.' The words came out in a gasp.

'You're tiring yourself, sir, and your wife'll blame me. I'll read a bit more of the paper, sir.'

A few minutes later, he noticed that Mr Greaves had fallen asleep, and he tiptoed out to tell Maggie Ryan that he was leaving. The poor old coot, he thought, as he went back to his work. He can't have much hope of getting better from the way he's talking. His mind must be wandering if he thinks I can buy him out.

Was the notion really so impossible? He did own a third share, and he still owned that block of land, which he knew had increased steadily in value. He would think about it for a while, and talk to Mr Greaves about it again when he seemed a little stronger.

It was on returning, tired, cold and muddy, from a bush trip that he found a little note left on the desk in the office informing him that Mr Greaves had died earlier that same day.

11

Christopher was genuinely sorry that Mr Greaves had died, for his liking for the older man had gone deeper than mere gratitude at being given a chance to better himself. After the funeral, he saw very little of the widow, for all his attention was given to the immediate problem of keeping the business going, and, as well, Mrs Greaves seemed to be avoiding him.

He soon heard that Mr Greaves had observed the traditional cutting off with a shilling, by leaving his son only a nominal sum, but the house, some other property, and two-thirds of the business had been left outright to Mrs Greaves. As soon as he decently could, Christopher discussed the possibility of buying out Mrs Greaves with her lawyer. Mrs Greaves informed him, through the lawyer, that she wanted things to continue as before, with Kershaw still on wages, and the profits being split three ways, with, of course, two-thirds going into the as yet unsettled estate.

It meant that he would continue to do one hundred per cent of the work and receive only thirty-three and one-third per cent of the reward. He had been prepared to abide by this whilst Mr Greaves was sick, but the idea of the arrangement continuing indefinitely did not please him at all.

He thought of selling his third, but knew quite well that he was unlikely to find a buyer who would take on such a badly weighted proposition. He could have kicked himself for not accepting Mr Greaves' offer immediately, and having it all tied up and in writing before his partner had died. After much consideration, he decided to discuss it directly with Mrs Greaves, and suggest that if she agreed to allow him to buy her out, she could reinvest in the firm at an interest rate to be fixed. In this fashion, he would have more capital, and she would profit by an addition to her income while still giving him the ownership he desired. Therefore, this being about two months after Mr Greaves' death, he sent her a letter asking if she would be so kind as to grant him a few minutes of her time. By the end of the week, he had received no reply, and he told himself that he should have known better than to expect favours from a snobbish woman who had things so much her way.

On the Saturday night following his note to Mrs Greaves, he dined with some friends at an hotel, Adelaide having gone on an overnight visit with her parents. For a while, he lingered on in the bar, exchanging jokes and gossip, but, inevitably, he had to excuse himself and go back to the store to check whether a team he half-expected had returned. It was unseasonably warm for October, and by the humidity he knew that it would most likely be raining by morning, and when he found that the team had not arrived, the teamster no doubt having decided to camp overnight, he felt restless.

He tried to read for a few minutes, but he felt like company, and resolved to go along to his favourite boxing saloon for a couple of hours. He knew from experience that some brisk sparring would wear out this feeling, and if afterwards he did wet his whistle with friends, he would be tired enough to come quietly home and go to bed. He was changing from his good frock coat into an old jacket when Mrs Greaves' Eurasian maid knocked on the door and, when he answered, handed him a note. She would, Mrs Greaves had written, be pleased to give him a few minutes, and he immediately sent back a message with the maid that he would be delighted to accept.

She must have been peeping out of the window, he thought, removing his jacket and replacing it with his best coat, and substituting the scarf he had knotted about his neck with his necktie. As an afterthought, just before leaving, he rinsed out his mouth with water, hoping to remove the odour of the liquor he had drunk earlier from his breath. Having thus prepared himself for the encounter, he walked past the vacant allotment to the Greaves' house, sparing a second to curse the mosquitoes which the early warmth had caused to breed by the million.

She greeted him in a low, formal voice, and invited him in, saying that she thought that there was a thunderstorm on the way. In spite of the warm evening, the parlour was stuffy from the heat of a good wood fire in the grate, and he observed that there was a bottle of wine and two glasses on a low table between two chairs. This cosiness made the hairs on the back of his neck prickle a warning, added to by his assessment of what she was wearing. As was proper, she wore unrelieved black, which suited her white skin and auburn hair, but although he was no authority on women's dress, he was certain that this trailing garment, unsupported by petticoats, trimmed with black lace, and bound at the waist by a sash, was more in the nature of a dressing-gown than an ordinary costume.

'Do sit down, Mr Kershaw,' she said, in a matter-of-fact manner, as she poured wine into two glasses. 'I've been wishing to talk with you.'

Then she seated herself on the pale blue sofa, her black silk rustling, and heavy-lidded eyes glittering at him across the rim of her glass. Out of politeness, he drank a little of his own wine, telling himself to be careful, as he did not wish to disgrace himself.

'But perhaps,' she continued, in a voice which was almost a purr, 'you'd best tell me first why you wished to see me.'

'It's about our business arrangement,' he said, and told her how he felt about the unfair situation which had arisen.

'Ah,' she said, finishing her wine and refilling the glass. 'I see.'

She half-reclined on the sofa, and he began to feel hot, uncomfortable, and scared.

'It's very warm in here, isn't it?' she added.

'Yes,' he gulped, and she smiled.

'If I leave the window open,' she went on, not taking her eyes from him, 'there is an unpleasant draught.'

How could she make this sound so suggestive?

'Would you consider selling out your share, Mrs Greaves?' he insisted, determined to obtain a firm answer.

She refilled her glass again, and topped his up, and he began to realise a few things about Mrs Greaves.

'It would suit me very well, Mr Kershaw.' She was half-way through the fresh glass. and showing no sign of it. 'I am thinking of returning to Britain. I didn't know whether you could raise the capital, but I didn't relish the idea of selling out over your head. After all, you've given so much to the business.'

And that is all I am going to give, he thought, but aloud he kept his tone level.

'I own a third, you know, and I think I can manage the rest.'

It was not exactly what he had wanted, for plainly she wished to take her money with her. Still, he was in no position to choose, and he did not really want Mrs Greaves as a partner.

'I'll talk to my lawyer on Monday.' Mrs Greaves fanned herself languidly, lifted her feet on to the sofa, and loosened her robe.

This was the signal for escape.

'Thank you for your time,' he said, jerkily, remembering the way she had fitted into his arms the day of Mr Greaves' second stroke, and George Forster's leering comment about virtue being its own reward.

'Thank *you*, Mr Kershaw.' She extended her hand to him. 'I'm so glad that we will part friends.'

Her hand was small and slim, and curled itself seductively into his palm.

'Of course, it's been difficult. A young man in your position, a widow in mine.' The hand remained a few moments longer, and was withdrawn, with an obvious unwillingness. 'It could so easily seem, Christopher, that we had designs upon one another.'

He was breaking out into a sweat. Her eyes seemed to be daring him to make the next move.

'But a handsome young man like yourself has other plans for a Saturday night!'

Was this dismissal or a challenge? Before he had to choose, she had reached out and pulled a bell-rope half-concealed by a curtain. The maid showed him out, and the cold, fresh air, blowing up in a sudden change from the sea, brought him to his senses. Phew!

By the time he reached the store, he was walking on air. He told himself not to feel so elated, but he was in a state to leap and yell for joy. He, Chris Kershaw, the dungaree kid, the poor stockman who had crawled into Melbourne with hardly a penny to his name, was now a man of property and affairs. As soon as he could, he would be removing the Greaves name from the sign and replacing it with his own.

As soon as it's all fixed, he thought, I'll ask Adelaide to marry me. A successful man needs a good wife to look after him. No more living here in a little room behind the store. Nothing very grand at first, a small cottage not too far away.

George Forster was very much in favour of marriage to Adelaide.

'Don't worry about the mother. Put your foot down as soon as the ceremony is over,' he advised.

'Eh!' protested Christopher. 'I haven't asked her yet.'

'Right girl for you,' said George, who, cynically opposed to marriage for himself, fancied himself as a matchmaker. 'Lucky you escaped that South Australian filly. Would have spent the rest of your life living up to her. Adelaide's just right. Not high and mighty, but she ain't common, either.'

Now that Mrs Greaves had made up her mind, she put her house up for sale and instructed her lawyer to arrange the sale of the two-thirds share to Christopher as quickly as possible. On Wednesday, Christopher interviewed a bank manager, who was so sympathetic that he decided to call on Adelaide that evening and tell her that obstacles were clearing away miraculously.

Half an hour after knocking on the Rosses' door, he was back in his own room, stunned and furiously angry. He had been refused entry. Miss Adelaide would not receive him, Mr Ross was apologetic, and yet stern. Plainly, he had been instructed by his wife to deal with their daughter's suitor.

'I'm sorry about this,' he said, in a mutter, 'but you've been a fool, and that's that. Adelaide's our only child. We've brought her up to expect certain standards. Don't blame you for sowing a few wild oats, but not if you're keeping company with our Adelaide.'

'What,' demanded Christopher, slowly, 'the hell are you talking about?'

'Don't use that tone of voice with me, young man. We took you on trust after that other — um — unfortunate — episode. Someone saw you Saturday night, Kershaw. Going into that Greaves woman's house and not leaving until daylight.'

'I was home by nine. I had to see her about some business.'

'People opposite are friends of Mrs Ross. They don't care much for Mrs Greaves. Like I said, they saw you going in, and heard a bit of a noise early in the morning, and looked out and saw you leaving.'

'It's a damned lie.'

'If you insist on using that sort of language, there's nothing more to be said. Goodbye.' But as he turned to go back inside, Mr Ross did have something more to say. 'You'll understand when you have children of your own.'

At this rate, thought Christopher, striding off in a temper, I won't be having any of my own. Why don't you lock the poor girl up in a convent and have done with it?

After walking the dark streets for a while, and nearly finding himself in a fight with two drunken shepherds who were engaged in drinking down their year's wages in a few days, he went home and forced himself to compose a cheerful letter to his family. Everything, he told them, was wonderful. The name Kershaw was going up in place of Greaves, and he did not have a worry in the world.

12

Kershaw, sitting in the first daylight of another densely hot day, could see, with hindsight, that Mrs Greaves had played a key part in those events leading to his marriage. Her sudden desire to leave New South Wales had handed him the chance to obtain complete control of the business, and the lover she followed had been the unknowing cause of the gossip which had lost him Adelaide.

Out of politeness, Christopher escorted the auburn-haired woman, whose secret life ran in such dark and devious channels, to Sandridge, on Port Phillip Bay, and went out to the ship with her. They stood on deck while Maggie Ryan set things to order in Mrs Greaves' cabin. Without much to say, they looked across the choppy water to the small jetty and scrub-covered sandhills, where only a few small buildings here and there indicated that this was the outer port of a thriving provincial town.

'It isn't much of a place. I'll be glad to return to civilisation,' she admitted, but as she spoke, her attention was not with him, but straying towards a tall and debonair man who was supervising the coming aboard of his wife and three young children.

Christopher knew him by sight. He was a military officer who had finished his time in Australia and was returning Home. The wife saw Mrs Greaves, and her face reflected dislike, fear, and sheer consternation, and in that instant Kershaw understood why Mrs Greaves had made up her mind to leave in such a hurry. This man was her lover, and near enough to his own height to be mistaken in dim light for himself by nosy neighbours fascinated by the comings and goings opposite.

He told George about it.

'Hell,' said George. 'Didn't you know? Thought all Melbourne knew about Mrs Greaves. Don't worry about the wife. If Mrs Greaves ain't too seasick, she'll soon find someone else. Remember Millie Hooper? Mrs Greaves is the same, only I heard a whisper she and that Hindu maid of hers were — um — not the way women should be towards one another.'

The two young men were strolling towards the saddling paddock at a race meeting being held just out of Melbourne, on the bank of the Saltwater River, a place which lent itself naturally to being used as a racetrack.

George had a half-share in one of the horses being raced, and after some discussion with the trainer, they turned to walk back to a vantage point to view the next race. It was then that George paused, and stared in the direction of a large party enjoying a picnic meal on the patchy grass.

'Chris, isn't that Arthur Ellis? Mr Watts' nephew — you overlanded with him.'

It was Arthur Ellis, much heavier than when he had excited girlish admiration in Adelaide back in '39. Close by was Estelle, still pretty, but somewhat harassed as two young children competed for her attention. A little apart, talking to a stout matron and a teenaged girl, was Laurie.

Christopher turned away, after glancing quickly over the men of the gathering, trying to guess which was Laurie's husband. Her charming laugh rang out as George walked across to the group. He introduced himself to Ellis and enquired after Mr Watts.

He was told that Mr Watts had now retired, fairly comfortably, in Sydney, having partly restored his fortune by a lucky investment in a whaling venture. As he spoke, Ellis glanced past George, with some curiosity, towards the tall young man who had remained some yards away. It was no wonder that he could not instantly identify Christopher Kershaw. His junior drover had grown taller and broadened out since those adventurous days when a simple expedition along the banks of the Murray invited attack from hostile tribesmen. As well, Kershaw, deeply in debt to the bank and often wondering whether he had over-reached himself, was now turned out smartly, if not elegantly, in the town uniform of light coloured trousers, dark frock coat, and tall hat. He was no longer so tanned, for the mistier Melbourne skies tended to keep skin pale for much of the year, and instead of being unshaven and untidy about the chin, he now sported well-barbered side whiskers.

'You remember Chris Kershaw, don't you?' asked George, gesturing towards his companion, who now felt Estelle regarding him coldly.

'Yes,' said Ellis, shortly, although he did seem surprised to see the other quite prosperous and presentable in appearance.

When Ellis had commenced talking to George, he had been affable, and in the natural course of things would

177

have introduced him to his wife and friends. Now his coolness was obvious even to one as brash as George Forster. Meanwhile, Kershaw knew that Laurie was staring at him, and he deliberately avoided meeting her eyes.

'What came over him?' demanded George, as the two retreated from this hostile atmosphere.

'His wife is Laurie Fenwick's sister. That isn't her name now, of course, but they haven't got over me daring to court one of their lot,' replied Christopher. The old familiar anger was coming over him again, the feeling of futility which gripped him when he came up against that invisible but steel-strong barrier. On his side were the lower orders: on theirs, the upper class, the better people, absolutely and utterly sure that Divine Providence had made them superior and ordained to be served by all others.

'Was *she* there? I saw a woman staring at you. Pretty little thing. Very fair hair, what you could see of it under that fool bonnet.'

'Yes. What the hell are they doing here? Ellis had a place out of Adelaide. Why did they come here? They belong in South Australia.'

'Doubt if Ellis *had* a place, old man. Managing for someone else, more like. No money. Plenty of side, but no blunt of his own. Now, stop worrying about them, and start praying that Sweet Sally'll win. I've five pounds on her nose.'

It was all very well for George Forster to talk. He had not been unexpectedly reminded of a love affair which had ended in humiliation and bitterly hurt feelings. That same night, as Kershaw checked through accounts by the light of a flickering lamp, he could not prevent his mind from straying back to that encounter on the racecourse.

How long had it been since they parted? Over three years, and in those three years the girlish prettiness had deepened into an ethereal beauty. It was hard for this young man, rough-raised and pragmatic, to think in similes, but Laurie was moonlight on a lake, mist on the mountains, golden sand seen through shallow water on a midsummer day, and just as hard to grasp.

She was married to another man, and he had best put her out of his mind, consoling himself with the thought that he had shown good taste by falling in love with her all that time ago. Like it or not, Laurie was going to occupy part of his heart for the rest of his days. Marrying Adelaide would have been no cure, and grossly unfair both to himself and the young woman.

★ ★ ★

'Kit?'

He had been called Kit by two persons in his life. One had been the master of ceremonies at that ill-fated boxing match, and the other Laurel Fenwick. He was watching a bullock team pull out of the yard, to the accompaniment of the ripe and fulsome language which teamsters considered necessary, when that low yet lilting voice caused him to swing round, to stare, almost open-mouthed. Laurie, fairness flattered by pale lilac and grey, stood framed in the doorway of the store. She must have asked to be shown through, he thought, wildly, wanting to run to her and snatch her into his arms.

'Hullo,' he said, calmly. 'I must apologise for the men's bad language. Now can I help you?'

That was the way to do it. Act in a polite, yet distant, fashion. It was all past, and he was not going to involve himself with another man's wife.

'I was passing and I saw your name up,' she said, and her voice faltered a little as she realised that she was unwanted.

'Oh. I'll be inside in a minute or two. Sit in my office.'

There. He had the upper hand. He had shown her that he was in no rush to talk with her, and he had ordered her to do something.

When he went into his tiny office, adjoining the room where he still slept in an attempt to save a pittance against his frightening mortgage, she was standing next to the window, and the morning sunshine caught at the fair hair arranged in a neat coil high on her head, for she had removed her bonnet. It was hot against the glass, and he could see the moisture on her forehead, beneath the hairline, and somehow this made her so very vulnerable.

'Your welcome was hardly warm, Kit,' she said, in a hurry.

'What did you expect?' His voice was as cold and brittle as he hoped it would be, and he saw her flinch. It gave him no satisfaction.

'When I saw you two days ago, at the races — and I had no idea you were living in Melbourne, Kit — I knew that I had to see you, to explain.'

'Why shouldn't I be living in Melbourne?'

'Edgar — Mr Broomhill, Jane's

husband — had cause to visit Melbourne soon after my marriage. I had asked him to see you — to . . . ' Her voice trailed off, and she stood bewildered and wordless, her air of helplessness emphasised by her tight-waisted, bell-skirted, sloping-shouldered dress, downward lines accentuated by the lilac inserts against the grey.

'I was away for a while. I visited my parents. But this is my home. There was no reason for me to leave for good. Your husband must be very understanding to let you call on old sweethearts like this. Still, that's the drill amongst your sort, ain't it? Marry to breed an heir, and then please yourself.'

She went very white, flushed, and then became white again.

'That,' she snapped, no longer meek and submissive, 'is quite the vilest thing any man ever said to a woman. You, Kit Kershaw, are a loathesome boor.'

She made to stalk out of the room,

but he barred her way, intent on revenge.

'Oh no,' he said, kicking the door shut behind him. 'You came here to start things again, and that's what you're getting.'

He grabbed her, without mercy, and pressed his mouth down on hers. For a moment, no more, she struggled, and then, with a delicious sigh, she yielded, and responded, without shame and without restraint. Her arms slid up about his neck, and the bonnet strings dropped from her fingers.

Yet, when he released her, it was not triumph he felt, but a rush of intense misery. God, how he wanted her, to go on kissing and embracing and caressing her until the ultimate consummation. How he had always wanted her, his dearest Laurie, who had been a sweet and forthright child, and was now the most enticing, desirable, beautiful and mysterious woman ever created. He knew that he was on a road from which there was no turning, and that she knew it too. They were going to become lovers, in every sense of the word.

'Kit,' she said, putting up a hand, in a typically feminine gesture, to make sure that her hair was still in place, 'you're a brute.' But she smiled as she spoke, and was in no hurry to leave, despite the brutish treatment she claimed to have endured.

She turned and bent down, to retrieve her bonnet, and while her face was away from him she addressed him again.

'Didn't you notice the way I'm dressed? I'm still in part mourning, Kit. My poor husband died eight months ago.' She straightened herself, and put her bonnet upon her head, and her voice trembled. 'Oh, Kit, he was such a kind man, and he suffered so much. I shall never understand why God caused him to have so much pain. And he was so brave!'

Once again she was in his arms, but this time he held her gently as she cried against his shoulder, comforting her by stroking her soft hair and murmuring softly to her.

'Do you know,' she said, when finally she drew away and accepted a loan of his handkerchief, 'that is the first time I've really cried since James died. Oh, Kit, the poor man! He faded away to nothing but skin and bones, and I know that he was in pain every minute. In the last weeks, Father gave him opium, but I don't think it helped very much. I stayed with him to the very end, Kit, because he had been so kind to me.'

'You're quick to get over it,' he snapped, trying to recover his senses.

'James took over our family debts, Kit. He was very much older — I was his third wife — and I could not feel about him as I would have my own choice. But I shall never regret the short time I gave him. I would never have betrayed him, Kit. You must believe that.'

He said nothing for a full minute, as his heart filled with a mounting anger against Dr Fenwick, whose fecklessness had caused his youngest daughter literally to sell herself to an ageing man who desired her sweet young body. When he did speak, he managed to sound light, almost casual.

'I'm a busy man during the day, Laurie. Can I call on you this evening?'

She replaced her bonnet at last, and as she tied the strings he saw that her grey eyes were tear-filled, although she was trying to blink away the droplets.

'I'm so glad you came, Laurie,' he added, dropping a kiss on her forehead. 'I wouldn't have come to you. You guessed that, I expect.'

She nodded, touched his cheek fleetingly with her fingers, and left with a quiet rustle of skirts. Her gentle fragrance of lavender water lingered for some minutes.

They were married three weeks later. He soon heard why Arthur Ellis, his family, and sister-in-law were in Melbourne. George had been partly right about Ellis's South Australian venture. Ellis, with little capital, had been manager and very junior partner on a property owned by English investors. Now he was to take up a similar position on a leased run about seventy miles west of Melbourne, for his superiors had decided to turn their South Australian land over to wheat-growing.

Ellis, thought Christopher sourly, had chosen his father-in-law well. A lot of talk, a lot of appearance, and very little hard cash. Not that he himself, he knew in those moments when he came down to earth from the euphoria which had engulfed him since Laurie had returned to his life, could brag. He had an enormous debt to the bank, and from the moment that Laurie allowed him to place his own ring on her finger, she would be penniless.

The late James Harden had adored his pretty young wife, and while he had been able, had indulged her to the extent of his resources. In spite of this, he was a realist. Laurie was bound to marry again, and he did not wish to see her the prey of a fortune-hunter. Therefore, her adequate, but by no means large, income ceased immediately she remarried, and the capital which had provided this income reverted to his children by his first marriage, and to a surviving brother.

George Forster told Christopher that he was a fool. He conceded that Laurie was pretty, and most fetching, but she was not their sort. After the first rush of hugging and kissing was over, they would have nothing in common.

On the other hand, Laurie's sister Estelle made it clear that she considered Laurie's new choice a disaster. He was a vulgar young man in trade, and the associate of another vulgar young man who ran a hotel and dabbled in colonial politics. It was definitely a great come-down after James Harden.

The wedding breakfast was provided by George, in the newly enlarged dining-cum-ballroom at his hotel. All things considered, the event went off very well, but it was noticeable that the guests formed two separate camps. The bridegroom's were culled from the strong anti-transportation faction so active in Melbourne, and the bride's from the socially superior squatting class, many of whom wanted cheap convict labour back as soon as possible.

Christopher was perhaps lucky that he was too happy to observe this. By a coincidence, he had that morning received a letter from his sister Joanna. Mails being what they were, the news of his impending marriage had not reached his family, but the tidings contained in Jo's neatly written epistle removed a persistent worry from his mind.

For years, he had dreaded that the Allards, Stephen and Percy, might direct their animosity towards Jo as she grew up into womanhood, and what Millie Hooper had told him about them added to his fear. But they had left the district, apparently for good. Old Captain Allard was now an invalid, so the two eldest sons had taken over the management of all his extensive interests, and this necessitated living close to Sydney.

It was comforting news on his wedding day, and augured a bright future.

13

Dr and Mrs Fenwick were appalled when they learnt that their daughter Laurel had finally married that impossible young man who had caused so much distress all those years before. They did not write directly to Laurie, but made it plain, through Estelle, that they no longer accepted her as a member of their family.

At first, the essential differences in the outlooks of the young couple did not matter very much. They were in love, they were creating a home, and Laurie's romantic yearnings were fulfilled. Outside events helped too, because there was a temporary lull in the running war over the transportation question, and Port Phillip's settlers, whether they be town or country folk, were united over another matter.

Back in 1840, less than five years

after this big area south of the River Murray, almost the same size as England, had been opened to white settlement, its few European inhabitants had decided that they resented being ruled from Sydney.

Sydney people, not wishing to lose population in this vast, empty country, rallied against separation, and Latrobe incurred lasting dislike amidst many Melburnians for not acting more resolutely. The issue simmered on for years, and when representative government was granted to New South Wales in 1843, the sheer inconvenience of sending Melbourne's elected members all the way to Sydney, with great personal waste of time and money, proved a further irritation to those to whom the Sydney-siders referred as 'cabbage-patchers'.

In desperation, Port Phillip people elected Sydney men to take care of their interests, and to the credit of those chosen, they stood by their duty to their faraway constituents.

One, a Dr Lang, drew up a suitable petition for separation which was sent to England. More time elapsed, but in 1846 it seemed that victory was in the hands of the 'cabbage-patchers', for the Imperial Government favoured passing the necessary Act of Parliament.

Alas, that government fell, and their successors ignored all those ins and outs which seemed so trifling to them and meant so much to the frustrated colonists of Australia's south-eastern corner. Then, when time rolled around for new elections, someone in Melbourne had a flash of brilliance. Instead of nominating a local candidate, why not choose a prominent British figure to represent Port Phillip in the Council? Earl Grey was nominated, and elected in one of the most bare-faced riggings in history. To his amazement, for he was not warned, he found that he was required to travel across the globe to Sydney, to sit in the small colonial legislature. Sick of jokes at his expense, he finally turned his attention to that fading petition, and separation became a certainty.

Port Phillip as a whole was now confident of success, but, like a nasty weed which seems to have been eradicated from the garden, but which in fact is flourishing in a hidden corner, transportation to the mainland once again was a possibility.

Life for Christopher Kershaw was full, with his business, his attendance at rallies devoted to these matters of public importance, and the social life which Laurie so enjoyed. At first, aware of his debts, he had been relieved that his pretty wife had not become pregnant straight away. He had always been secretly glad that she had borne no children by her first husband, but it was not until two years had passed that he began to suspect that she might be barren.

By the third year of their marriage, Laurie had a well-established circle of friends in Melbourne, and now the first rifts appeared. Her looks and breeding made her popular within that circle which centred about the Melbourne Club and the Superintendent's charming little house on Jolimont Hill. Her husband found himself more and more of an outsider. He trusted Laurie, or so he told himself, but she was pretty and lively, and when his business took him away into the bush for days on end he was haunted by jealous fears and suspicions which he tried to convince himself were groundless. Then, unexpectedly, an ally, and guardian of his treasure, appeared.

Hughie Deane, Old Cornstalk, arrived one day while Christopher was having a noisy argument with a teamster who had allowed several oxen to become so hopelessly bogged that they had had to be destroyed.

'Hullo, Young Cornstalk,' said the old bushman, just as if they had parted the previous day. 'Having trouble?'

'Bloody fool,' snarled the other. 'Should have broken his neck for him.

Where did you come from?'

'Oh, jest blew into town for a spell,' replied Deane airily, but now that Kershaw had recovered his temper and was taking in his old companion, he could see that Deane was run down and miserable in appearance, and the slight limp which had been barely noticeable at their last meeting after Mrs Dalgarno's temperance rally, had worsened.

'Staying long?' Christopher sounded casual, being aware that a too apparent show of interest was considered bad taste amongst the men of the bush.

'I dunno yet,' said Hughie Deane, cagily, but the younger man's shrewd gaze had already noticed the anxiety in the other's pale irises, and he guessed that his old friend had reached the sad but inevitable end of the itinerant bush worker's life. Deane was no longer fit enough for the harsh and demanding conditions, and now faced the prospect of building himself a little hut somewhere not too far out of town, and eking out an existence as best he could, with a dog or two for company.

He had to put it carefully, so as not to offend Hughie Deane with any hint of charity, but it was not charity which he had in mind. It was a watchdog.

They negotiated cautiously. He had recently moved into a larger house in Collins Street, with a larger yard, which needed more looking after. There was a living-in maid, but she was a silly, nervous girl, and it worried him sick when he was away to think of so many of those old lags still hanging about Melbourne, with more forever sneaking over from Van Diemen's Land. If he had someone he could trust . . . and there were odd jobs at the store, too.

Deane hummed and ha'ed. He did not fancy town life, and there was talk of a droving job, but he reckoned a fellow had to settle down sometime. So they shook hands on it.

Of course, Christopher did not expect Hughie Deane to act as a spy, but he judged that the older man's presence somewhere about his home would discourage any one of those dashing young squatters or army officers from pushing luck further. Thus, he gave his jealousy a fillip by admitting that it existed, although his fears about the 'old hands' who abounded in Melbourne were shared by most of the respectable population.

It was about this time that the transportation question came again to the fore, stirred up by the arrival of persons promptly nicknamed 'The Pentonvillains'. In an attempt to please those who wanted cheap labour, and at the same time avoiding the prickly anti-transportation element, English authorities sent out a batch of paroled men, selecting prisoners who had shown signs of reform. Some of these ticket-of-leave men did make a fresh start and quietly faded away into the mainstream of Australian life. Too many were lively scoundrels who quickly dropped all pretence of reform when they sized up the possibilities of life under the Southern Cross.

Then the news arrived. Westminster had given in to the pleas of the squatters, and was despatching convicts who were simply that. The citizens of Sydney and Melbourne forgot their natural animosity towards each other, and united in a series of enraged protests. George Forster, one of the most vehement opponents of the Pentonville scheme, once again began distributing leaflets and posters, and exhorting everyone he met to add their signatures to petitions.

Christopher's interest was not entirely altruistic, although he detested the 'old hands' he often had to employ, and had had more than enough of their thieves' cant, their unreliable ways and their unquenchable thirsts. All that could be hoped, he told George over a quiet glass of ale, was that they'd eventually all die off, provided they were not replaced.

Like many others, he also held hopes that once the stigma of transportation was lifted from New South Wales, the trickle of free immigrants would increase to a large flow. The sort of progress he wanted could come only with more population, and progress was not a grand going forward of the country as a whole, but the expansion of his own business and the easing of his financial worries. Hopes of settling his enormous debt to the bank were constantly confounded by static conditions, and, hard though it was to admit this to himself, his mode of living.

His attitude to his wife was strongly coloured by the urge that he had to show her family that Laurie had done well for herself by marrying him. He did not realise that, by pandering to his own pride in this way, he was encouraging those less attractive traits in her character. To keep up with the circle in which she had made her friends, she had to spend fairly extravagantly, and so it was that on quarter days he paid his interest and very little off the main body of his debt.

Underlying all this, there was another reason he longed to see the end of transportation. Stephen Allard had recently been elected to the New South Wales Legislative Council, and it was notorious that he was a supporter of transportation. Anything which was against Stephen Allard had to be good.

What with meetings and deputations, he began spending evenings away from home, and Laurie soon complained that she was being denied the chance to attend the evening parties and subscription balls which formed such a large part of her life. In the highest society of London, wives and husbands could be escorted quite safely by others than their own spouses, but in provincial Melbourne such behaviour would cause a veritable cloudburst of gossip.

'I'm sorry, dearest,' he said, bending over and kissing her crown of light hair, 'but this is important to us all. As soon as we've won the battle, you'll have so much of my company you'll be sick of it.'

And underneath this loving assurance, he thought that it was worth enduring her pouts and complaints to be spared that dreadful chewing jealousy he experienced when she received the attention of other men.

Laurie, who was embroidering one of those pieces of uselessness upon which women set such store, looked up with a certain stoniness.

'Some of our friends are squatters, Kit,' she said.

'Your friends,' he retorted.

It was the first time the rift between them had shown itself so obviously. No more was said that night, but the divergence was there, in the open. For Laurie, the squatters represented the upper class, the Australian counterpart of the solid land-owning families at Home, who, however their fortunes fluctuated, were still the élite. They

203

could have faults, do wrong, and go blatantly against public interest, but to a young woman of Laurie's upbringing they were Best People.

Her husband was hurt and worried, the more so because he could understand her point of view. She had more in common with the wives of the class which would benefit from a resumption of transportation than with the womenfolk of the tradesmen and artisans who made up the bulk of the town population. Painfully, too, he felt the unspoken implication.

You would not be here, Kit, if there had been no transportation.

14

After the convict ship *Hashemy* sailed into Port Phillip Bay early in 1849 and was sent on its way, Superintedent Latrobe sent orders to the pilot station at the entrance to the almost landlocked bay. Any convict ship arriving off the Heads was to be refused entry through the narrow passage, but, nevertheless, the *Randolph* slipped through during bitterly cold weather in August and anchored off the mouth of the Yarra Yarra. Hundreds of irate inhabitants, amongst them George Forster and Christopher Kershaw, assembled on the chilly shore, huddling and stamping against the icy wind. Kershaw could see the bright coats of the marines on board, and the glint of their arms, and for a while it seemed as if the issue might be forced. Eventually, the captain, fearing bloodshed if he attempted to land his unwanted goods, ordered the anchor up, and the ship and its unhappy cargo lurched off through the greyly swelling waves towards the Port Phillip Heads, sixty miles away, and, ultimately, to Sydney. Some time later, Melbourne's newspapers reported that angry demonstrations made it impossible to land the convicts there, and the wretched felons, to whom the voyage must have seemed an endless nightmare, were taken several hundred miles north and dumped at tropical Moreton Bay.

That beach, thought Kershaw, riding back to town with George along a track which wended through dense scrub, was as cold as Laurie has been over this business.

It was in this atmosphere of increasing strain that they attended a soiree during December of that year. In between musical items, she immediately annoyed him by attracting the attention of a tall, redheaded man of about her husband's age. He was recently out from Britain, Scotland to be precise, and, as usual, talk soon turned to the shortcomings of his new land, with Laurie at her sweetest and most vivacious. It was hard to credit, when one heard her talk so enchantingly, with a certain flutter of the fan, that she had left England at the age of ten and had to stretch her memory to recall all those things about which homesick colonists made such a fuss.

As Christopher quietly seethed, a hand touched his sleeve, and turning, he was surprised to see George, who avoided such things as musical soirees like the plague.

'What are you doing here?' he whispered, and Forster grinned.

'You'd be surprised where I've been tonight,' he replied. 'Not here socially,' he went on, in a low voice, with a look which held more than a hint of disapproval in Laurie's direction. Forster and young Mrs Kershaw nodded at one another with their usual barely concealed dislike, and, the piano striking up again to signal the return to entertainment, the two friends went outside into the garden to continue their discussion.

'Another transport off the Heads,' explained George. 'Pilot at Queenscliff has orders not to bring her in. Another showdown, Chris. You'd think Westminster'd have more sense by now. Can't they get it into their thick aristocratic heads the way we feel?'

'Do you think the master'll try to come in without a pilot?'

The passage from Bass Strait through the Heads, known as The Rip, was treacherous, but not impossible to a skilled navigator.

'Depends on the master's orders. That's why I wanted to see you, Chris. We've chartered the *Radcliffe* to take us down to Queenscliff from Coles' Wharf. Six tomorrow morning. Bring a gun. If the *Adelaide* comes through The Rip we'll fire a few shots into the air to let the master know we mean business.'

'I'll be there,' promised Kershaw,

without hesitation. 'I'll offend some of Laurie's friends, but that's too bad.'

'If you don't mind me saying so, do more than offend some of 'em. Know that redheaded fellow?'

'No. Never seen him before. Some squatter in town for a spell, I expect.' He had no intention of letting on to George how much Laurie's habit of flirting upset him.

'He's in town waiting for a berth to Sydney. Marrying the Allard girl at Christmas. I hear most of the gossip in my line of business, Chris. Girl's apple of her father's eye, only seventeen. Fellow down from Sydney talking about it today. Rumour is girl is desperate to leave Sydney. Scandal hushed up all this time, but Stephen had a row with one of the servants, and he's put it about. Mrs Allard shot Captain Allard. Trying to do away with herself again, and he tried to take the gun from her. Crippled for life. Then, while everyone was rushing about, she locked herself in another room and finally did it. Overdose of laudanum. Ramsay, the redheaded fellow, leases a run in partnership with the Allards. Out Macedon way, I think.'

He referred to Mount Macedon, about thirty miles north of Melbourne. As he spoke, Christopher closed his eyes for a moment, seeing again the smart carriage in Bathurst's bare and muddy square, the two little boys in silk caps, the distinguished gentleman on horseback, and the elaborately dressed lady. Then, he heard those whispers between his parents in the night. They had been afraid. Afraid of the Allards. And superimposed was the picture of a patch of blue sky, surrounded by faces, as he lay on his back in the dirt, knocked down by Stephen Allard. For so long, he had feared that the Allard malevolence might touch his sister Joanna, but instead, it was reaching back towards him through Laurie.

'Six at Coles' Wharf,' repeated George. 'Feeling all right? Looked a bit queer there for a moment.'

'I'm all right. Goose walked over my grave. I'll see you in the morning.'

Christopher managed to insinuate himself back into the chair alongside his wife during a pause between the songs being delivered by a young woman with a quavering soprano.

'We have to leave,' he whispered in his wife's ear. 'I have to be up at five.'

She was not pleased, but neither did she want to make a scene in front of her friends. On the way home she made her feelings plain.

'How could you be so rude, Kit? I know you don't care for anything more illuminating than boxing and horses and horrid political meetings, but it would not have hurt you to have *endured* a little longer.'

'There's another convict transport off the Heads, and we must make sure she doesn't come any further in towards Melbourne.'

'But, Kit, tomorrow is Sunday, and we are going on a picnic after church.

Surely you remembered.'

'I'm sorry, Laurie. I forgot about the picnic when George told me about the transport. Try to understand that it's important to stop those convicts being landed here. Those people back in England make our laws, but they don't understand what it's like here.'

Laurie walked alongside him, chin in air, just far enough away to stop him holding her arm.

'It seems to me,' she said, haughtily, changing the subject slightly as she always did when worsted in an argument, 'that you associate far too much with Mr Forster. From what I've heard since, I deeply regret that he arranged our wedding breakfast.'

'George ain't the type I'd take into Sunday school,' admitted her husband, angrily, 'but he's done a damned sight more for this town than some of those swells you're so stuck on. And it would please me, while we're on the subject of friends, if you don't go out of your way to speak to that fellow Ramsay again.'

'Oh?' The maid had left a lamp burning in the hallway of their house, and it illuminated the stern expression which had settled upon Laurie's usually vivacious little face as she removed the gauzy scarf which protected her hair.

'Yes.' He had dug in his heels too, and rashly, instead of explaining the reasons for his sudden objection to a young man who had done no more than utter a few pleasantries to his wife, he demanded her absolute obedience. There was more than more jealousy involved this time. His parents had been servants to the Allards, and he had been humiliated by Stephen Allard.

'And why? Because, no doubt, he has the wisdom to see that we can't have any civilisation worth mentioning unless we also have men to build the roads and other things we need.'

'That's a lot of . . . ' He stopped in time, and amended what he was going to say. 'That's the way his lot talk. All they want is cheap labour for themselves.'

'You've never travelled, Kit. You cannot dream how backward this town is.'

'Well, so far,' he drawled, 'I ain't had to leave a country and find another place to live because I couldn't pay my debts there.'

This went straight home. Laurie could admit that her family were singularly inept in money matters, but having it tossed into her face was something else.

'Go on your horrid expedition. *I* shall go on my picnic.'

★ ★ ★

'They're going!'

Someone cried out the words, and all eyes strained towards the *Adelaide*. The anchor was being weighed, the sails were shaking out, and the ship was turning about. For the men on the cliffs, this was victory, and they cheered wildly, jumping up and down in their exultation. It was, they could

214

boast to the end of their lives, the last convict transport despatched to the eastern part of mainland Australia, and they had sent it on its way.

For Christopher, the larger drama was over, but the more personal, painful part was ahead. He arrived home late, tired but triumphant, from the expedition to Queenscliff, and found his wife sitting up in bed, entrancing under her little lace-edged nightcap, making a pretence of reading by the light of the lamp on the bedside table. She was not as calm as one would have expected: her bosom was heaving slightly as if she had just taken part in some exertion.

'Oh, home already?'

'No, I'm still out on the bay.'

'I cannot bear sarcasm. Nor the smell of liquor.'

He had had a couple of shots of rum on the way back, both in the cause of celebration and of warmth, for in spite of it being the summer month of December, it had been cold out on the water. Plainly, she was in one of those irksome moods of hers, but he had something of his own to say.

'How long have you been in bed?'

'Quite a while.'

'No more than a few seconds, I'll lay.'

He was angry to the point of fury, and after trying to keep calm and in control of the situation, he was pushed over the edge into rage by her cool monosyllable.

'Oh?'

'You're lying. I saw you myself. I was two hundred yards up the street, and I saw you plain as daylight. It's full moon tonight, remember. You were left at the gate by that Ramsay fellow. I passed him. Much as I could do not to knock his confounded head off.'

'What are you suggesting?'

'I'd say that this picnic of yours lasted a damned sight longer than it should have. It's a funny thing this happened the night when Hughie

Deane isn't here at the house, but acting as a nightwatchman at the store because Harry is sick.'

There was a long silence.

'I see,' she said, after a while. 'I hadn't realised that Mr Deane reported all my comings and goings to you. Thank you, Kit, for being so trustful.'

At a time like this, the store was his haven, and he spent the rest of the night, sleepless and uncomfortable, on a heap of folded blankets of the sort he supplied as standard equipment for shepherds and other pastoral workers. The store was the one place where he was the superior in a world which was designed to keep him inferior. That was the dreadful part of it. No matter how he worked, or how much he got on, he could not match the Fenwicks, the Ramsays, and the Allards of the world. The small victory of the day, seeing the *Adelaide* sail off, which at the time had seemed a signal defeat for the Allards and their whole ilk, was nothing when set against the great blazing triumph of

217

the Allard-Fenwick alliance in ruining his life.

When he was a small boy, his father had allowed him to raise and tame a small wallaby he had found in the bush, abandoned by its mother when fleeing hunters. For a while, the animal had been his close playmate, but one day, when he was doing his small duties about the farm, with Joey plomping along beside him, he had seen a pair of wallabies standing, their small silly front legs limp, their dark pointed ears pricked up, at the edge of the bushland, curious, yet ready to bound off at the slightest threatening move on his part. With a childishly breaking heart, he had watched Joey hop in the direction of the strangers, pause, look back once, and then thump off as if he had never left his fellows. Moments later, the trio had vanished into the heavy lower growth of the uncleared land beyond the farm.

In a way, it was the same with Laurie. He had succeeded, for a while, in keeping her from her own kind. He had done his best. His debt to the bank had not been reduced as quickly as it should have been over the past twelve months because of his heavy domestic expenses. He knew quite well that they spent too much and that frugality was necessary, but always, he felt under an obligation to impress Laurie. She had to have pretty dresses and other trifles so that she could meet her friends on an equal footing, she wanted to go here, she wanted to go there. He could not refuse her, although he knew that the more she mixed with those friends who meant so much to her, the more she would see him as he really was, uncouth, and largely uneducated.

If only I could become rich, he thought. Really rich. Nothing else would matter then.

His start on the business of the new week was tardy, and not helped by several callers who wished to talk over the implications of the *Adelaide*'s departure. They all saw this as a good omen for the future. Immigrants, they believed, would be eager to come to New South Wales now that the bad odour attached to transportation was all but dispersed. The last visitor before midday was George Forster, and he astonished his heavy-eyed friend by compressing into just two sentences the very reasons why immigrants to New South Wales would still be few and cautious.

'Well, Chris, I've made up my mind. I'm off to California to try my hand at digging for gold.'

Kershaw could only gape at him. True, for months there had been a steady trickle of men leaving Australia for the Eldorado on the other side of the Pacific Ocean, ever since the startling news of huge gold finds near a dozing Spanish hamlet called San Francisco had reached Sydney. But George was wealthy these days, and had no need to answer the mad call of gold.

'Look at it this way, Chris,' Forster continued, smiling a little at the expression on the other's face. 'I'm nearly thirty. I feel like a bit of adventure before I get too fat and comfortable. One of my nephews up in Sydney is going, and I'm keeping an eye on him.'

So there it was. George, well supplied with worldly goods, could not resist the lure of gold. How then could anyone expect those less fortunately placed to put aside the chance of 'striking it rich' in exchange for hard work, a small cottage, and the chance of mutton three times a day?

15

Estelle, Laurie's sister, was expecting another child in January, and as she was feeling tired and poorly, Laurie travelled to the Ellis's homestead to keep her company. That was the official reason for her absence, but although neither really admitted it, Mr and Mrs Kershaw knew that Estelle's forthcoming confinement provided a good excuse for a separation.

Christopher rode the seventy miles west to join the Ellis family for Christmas, without any real enthusiasm. He saw them perhaps twice a year, for Laurie's sake, and had felt that was sufficient. His wife had felt the break with her family very keenly, and although she and Estelle had never been close, her eldest sister's mild defiance of parental edicts meant a great deal to her.

Just after dawn on Boxing Day, Arthur Ellis and Christopher went out with their guns in the hope of shooting a bustard or two to implement the larder. They were not in luck, for already the heavily built, incredibly stupid native 'turkeys' were becoming rare, victims of the white man's more sophisticated weapons and unconcern for the regeneration of the species.

'I believe you helped chase the *Adelaide* away,' said Ellis, as the two men returned to the horses left tethered in the shade of a clump of huge old trees.

'Yes.' The younger man did not wish to discuss the matter. Arthur Ellis was a squatter, one of 'them'.

'Glad to hear of it. I've never mentioned it before, but I'm awkwardly placed here. Some of my neighbours signed the petitions, and I've been odd man out. And, Kit, anything which puts Steve Allard's nose out of joint suits me. Steve made my uncle's life unbearable up there at Bathurst, you know, after the crash, when he managed the place while the Allard boys learnt the ropes. I'll owe that the old Captain was decent enough, but Steve was a young swine. Now Steve is backing old Charlie Wentworth, I hear, so that there'll be a peerage in this country. Imagine it. Lang put it in a nutshell. The dunghill aristocracy!'

Suddenly, the two men, so long wary and separated by memories of that journey overland years before, when the gulf between the expedition's leader and a young drover had been so wide, grinned at each other, and laughed.

On the way back to the homestead, Ellis delicately broached the subject of his sister-in-law. According to Estelle, the girl had always had her head in the clouds, and full of romantic nonsense. If poor old James Harden hadn't died when he did, he would have eventually had his hands full with her. There was no harm in Laurie, really. It was just that, well, she found it hard to settle down to a humdrum life. It was a pity she hadn't had children. That would have steadied her and given her something to think about besides herself.

'Don't worry. I'll send her home when the baby's here and Estelle's lying-in is over,' added Arthur Ellis. 'And when I have the chance, I'll talk to her about Ramsay and the Allard girl. As I said, Kit, I've no reason to like the family either, and I've the advantage of not being a jealous brute as she says you are.'

It all went to prove, thought Kershaw many months later, arising from his hot and sticky chair under the veranda roof to go inside for a cool shower before beginning the day, that friends turn up in unexpected places. Laurie returned home the same week as the newly-wed Mr and Mrs Ramsay passed through Melbourne, but for a reason she did not divulge to her husband, the welcoming party she had promised did not eventuate.

As for their relationship at that

time, although reconciliation was not complete, life went along smoothly through the long summer days, with evenings spent out of doors, and pleasant excursions to the seaside, or by small steamer up the Yarra Yarra. As often happens in those latitudes, the most prolonged spell of warm weather was in March, during the days of the equinox, when the days were so balmy, the evenings so mild, the heavens so clear, the stars so huge and bright of a night, that it seemed impossible that there would ever again be cold winds and driving rain.

As March ended, the prolonged summer became wearisome. The water, carted from the Yarra Yarra, was muddier than ever. Flies hung about in their myriads, and the stench from the boiling-down works flavoured the air unpleasantly. Riding back into Melbourne just on sunset, when the dark thunder clouds were trimmed briefly with a golden edging, Kershaw made up his mind that when things improved (when?) they would shift out of town into one of the new suburbs. He reached his house on foot, having left his horse in the stables at the store, an arrangement he preferred, as it kept the smells and flies away from home. He was tired and dusty, and looking forward to removing his riding boots, having a cold wash, and perhaps sitting outside for a while with a cool drink.

The house was very quiet, and almost as soon as he entered, Gladys, their only living-in servant, came out from the kitchen and waylaid him.

'Oh, Mr Kershaw,' she said, 'Missus is in ever such a state. Wouldn't touch a bite, she wouldn't; just went into the bedroom and bin there ever since, she has, sir.'

'How long ago?'

'Oh, about half past four, sir. Came home all of a hurry, she did, and just ran into your bedroom and slammed the door.'

'Thank you.'

Gently, he opened the door to

their bedroom, and peered inside. Laurie's bonnet, tossed towards a chair, had missed, and lay untidily on the floor, alongside her reticule, and the pretty little pink parasol, which she carried so faithfully in sunny weather to protect her complexion. Laurie herself lay diagonally across the bed, a mass of crumpled skirts and loosened hairpins. He leaned over, and touched her. His first thought that she had been taken suddenly ill, with one of the many ailments flourishing about Melbourne, was dispersed by her shuddering response.

'L-leave me alone. Just leave me alone!'

'You'd best tell me what's wrong.' He sat alongside her, and was shocked to see, in the remaining faint light seeping through the curtains, that her face was swollen with weeping.

'I want to die. I've never, never been so humiliated! I'll never, never be able to go out again.'

'What happened? Tape come out of

your petticoat in the street?'

The whole tragedy was now spelled out, with more sobs and declarations of despair. Laurie had been at a tea party being held to discuss means of raising money for the assistance of destitute female immigrants, and had been introduced to young Mrs Ramsay, *née* Allard, who was in town for a few days. Then, out of the blue, it came. Mrs Ramsay refused to be introduced.

'Listen,' he said, holding her close, 'she's an Allard, and they're all as mad as hatters. From what George Forster told me, her mother was so close to being a lunatic that it didn't matter.'

She apparently did not hear him, but babbled on.

'Oh, how could I have been so stupid? I insisted that she explain her behaviour, because she can be no more than seventeen. She looked me up and down, in the horridest way, Kit, and said . . .'

'I know. As if she had a rotting bullock carcass a yard from her nose.

That's the Allard style.'

'She said to Mrs Pearce, 'I'm afraid I am going to find your Melbourne ways very strange, Mrs Pearce. In Sydney, emancipists or their families are never allowed into the best drawing-rooms.' If only I'd kept my head, Kit, and had ignored her, but I demanded that she apologise, and she looked at me, still in that horrid fashion, and said, 'Why, Mrs Kershaw?' and *someone else laughed*.'

The tears began to fall again, and he thought back to his own ultimate humiliation of lying on the dirt there in Bathurst, looking up at a circle of faces and hearing Stephen Allard's sneering laughter. He felt the anger eating inside, and the old bafflement which had lingered on through the intervening years filled him. Yet, when he spoke, it was lightly.

'There can't be many people in any drawing-room in Sydney at that rate. I could name a dozen families who wouldn't be let in, and they're as rich as Croesus these days!'

Poor, silly Laurie, he thought, all those months later, as he dressed for the day's business on that blazingly hot Wednesday morning. For days, she had moped at home, hardly daring to go out on the most ordinary errands, for fear of being the butt of more mockery. For the first time in her life, the self-assurance which, occupied with her attractive looks, had made her the popular centre of a select circle, was faltering.

Half-way through the fourth year of her second marriage, she was pregnant, and sickly with it. Now she needed all the devotion he was able to offer, and during the long, wet and dreary winter, when the Yarra Yarra burst its banks and flooded low-lying land near the town, he despaired of her living to see another summer. Estelle, alarmed by her sister's state of health, wrote to her parents in Adelaide, and managed to affect a reconciliation between Laurie and the older Fenwicks. There was talk, for a while, of Mrs Fenwick travelling to Melbourne, but Dr Fenwick fell prey to a mild stroke in September, which made this impossible.

Yet, despite the glum and gloomy winter, there was a cheerful atmosphere abroad in Melbourne and throughout the Port Phillip District. During September, 1850, it had become obvious that within a short time official intelligence of the passing of the long-awaited Separation Act back in Britain would reach Melbourne. After a decade of squabbling and scheming, the settlers south of the River Murray would be able to run their own affairs free of Sydney. Now, with the great moment imminent, plans were made for a suitable celebration. Immediately the news was received, a Royal Salute would be fired and, in the evening, signal fires would be kindled on hilltops so that the information could spread speedily from point to point across the new State. The fourth day after this would be a public holiday.

By a lucky coincidence, the new stone bridge across the Yarra Yarra, Prince's Bridge, was almost completed, and what better way of expressing loyalty to the Queen than to open officially this edifice named after her elder son?

Ultimately, the great day was the 15th of November, 1850. For once, Melbourne's notoriously fickle weather was kind, and the day dawned balmy and sunny. However, even as they prepared to leave the house, Laurie complained that she felt unwell again, and urged Christopher to attend the ceremony without her. The baby was due about Christmas, and even her determined fondness of social occasions could not cope with both the heaviness of her body and a feeling of malaise.

After some hesitation, her husband left, promising to be back within two hours.

It was very much a gala occasion, brightened as much by the uniforms of the military as by the ladies' dresses. Another picturesque feature was provided by the presence of the native mounted police, splendid in their gaudy green outfits trimmed with 'possum fur.

The Superintendent, Charles Joseph Latrobe, Esquire, one of the best-looking men ever sent to Australia as an administrator, gazed over the assemblage with pride. He had seen this settlement struggle forward from a collection of huts and tents to become an established town of twenty thousand people, serving an area, the size of England, which had a population of about seventy thousand all told. When the Act of Separation became a legal fact, halfway through 1851, he would become Lieutenant Governor, a reward of sorts for a long term during which he had been bitterly criticised by many of those whose welfare he had at heart.

Kershaw stood with some friends near the well-mounted native troopers, and tried to concentrate on the endless speeches. For a town of its small size, Melbourne was well supplied with orators, and the young man decided that, as soon as decently possible, he would slip away. Laurie's strained appearance had worried him.

Then he began to have the feeling that someone was staring at him, and in the end, he could not resist glancing over his shoulder. Almost immediately, he saw Stephen Allard glaring in his direction as if wishing him to shrivel away to nothing. At his side was Percy, and close by, two youths, aged about fourteen and sixteen respectively, who by their physiognomy could not have been other than Allards, for theirs was a tribe into which new members arrived stamped from the same mould, birth after birth.

The elder Allards nudged the younger ones, and nodded towards Christopher, and they all examined him dispassionately, taking in his tall beaver hat, dark brown frock coat worn over pale fawn inexpressibles, his polished city boots, and finding under all this superficial improvement, the same old cornstalk Chris Kershaw.

Percy had not changed much over the years, and still had the weak look about the chin and the air of one who never quite made up his mind for himself. Stephen was heavier than Kershaw remembered, and now that he no longer led the hard-riding outdoor life of a squatter, there was about him a certain flabbiness which made him appear much older than his years. His face had the reddened skin of a heavy drinker, and although the day had not yet progressed very far, it was obvious that he had already consumed sufficient to make him reckless.

'The air's foul near the Yarra Yarra,' he announced, in a loudly carrying voice. 'To hear these cabbage-patchers[1] talk, you'd think they all came out of the top drawer, but there's as much

_____

[1] Melburnians.

convict scum down here as there is up in Sydney.'

Kershaw turned his back, but others, always hypersensitive over disparaging references to Melbourne by Sydney visitors, stared at the Allards with a curiosity which threatened to turn into violence. The more timid and discreet of the ladies in the vicinity moved away with a rustle of best petticoats, or clung more firmly to the arms of their menfolk.

'When you look at these fellows, all dressed up like respectable men, you'd never guess that their mothers had been convict harlots.'

Christopher told those near to him, quietly, that he was leaving on account of Mrs Kershaw's poor health that morning.

'Mrs Kershaw, eh?' laughed Stephen, moving closer. 'Now I wonder which English gaol *spewed* her out.'

As he uttered these words, he planted his hefty frame squarely in front of the man he had insulted.

'You're not only scum. You haven't the guts to stick up for your women,' added Allard, and lunged at Christopher.

Kershaw dodged nimbly to one side, at the same time removing his best hat and handing it to the nearest onlooker. In the near distance, the deliverer of the eulogy on the new state's many virtues was now reading out some doggerel which had been composed in honour of the occasion.

'Many are all Victoria's Youth
And charming, as her glorious
    clime.'

It is doubtful whether those standing near the two combatants heard this sweeping praise as they cleared a space in anticipation of more down-to-earth entertainment.

'For love of freedom famed, and
    Truth!
Country and sons are in their
    prime!'

The genteel applause which greeted this was almost instantly strengthened by cheers as a well-delivered left fist smashed against Stephen Allard's jaw.

> 'Rule Victoria — Australia rules
>   the waves —
> Victoria's sons will ne'er be slaves.'

A roar attended these fine sentiments, which coincided with the thump, as reeling back, Stephen Allard carried his brother Percy with him to the ground.

Calm of expression as he rubbed his smarting knuckles, Kershaw inwardly exulted at the astonishment on Stephen's face. He retrieved his hat, not wishing to continue the fight, and observing a plump constable forcing his way through the fascinated crowd.

But, the next instant, the two younger Allards hurled themselves against him, and all three fell in a struggling heap. For some moments, the two lads rained blows on him until they were dragged away, and Kershaw was able to scramble to his feet, glancing meanwhile down at his besmirched clothes.

'That man attacked my brother!' squawked Percy, as the constable demanded to know the cause of this disturbance. 'My brother is Stephen Allard, Esquire, and a member of the New South Wales Legislature, and I demand that . . .'

'Excuse me.'

The interloper was a slim man in early middle age, whose prematurely grey hair beneath his tall hat added to, rather than detracted from, his well-bred good looks. He smiled at Kershaw, who dabbed at a swelling left eye with his handkerchief, while Stephen Allard, groaning, raised himself to a sitting position, and tenderly touched his jaw.

'This man,' continued the newcomer, whom Kershaw had recognised as a Mr Andrew M'Kirk, a magistrate, 'is a respected and respectable business man here in Melbourne, but within the hearing of a great many people, including myself, he was grossly insulted without cause by the — the *gentleman* on the ground.' He indicated Stephen with the tip of his cane. 'The blame lies entirely with you, sir,' he added, addressing Stephen directly. 'Take my advice, sir, and return quietly to your lodgings and sober up.'

'Why, you!' Stephen's high-coloured face became even more florid. 'Who the hell do you think you're addressing?'

'You are addressing a Melbourne magistrate,' was the curt answer.

The Allards, realising that they had come up against a wall of local unity, went off grumbling and muttering. Christopher, who had also had enough, put his hat back on his head, and, painfully aware of his left eye, which was almost closed, left the scene. His triumph at having avenged himself over his Bathurst defeat all those years ago was dimmed by the thought of having to face his wife's disapproval. She never made any secret of her feelings about his custom of spending an occasional hour sparring in a boxing saloon.

As it happened, she was quite willing to accept his explanation that he had been knocked over by a trooper's horse, for when he arrived home it was to find that she was in the early stages of labour.

16

George Forster turned up again on a hot Sunday afternoon in January, 1851. Christopher was trying to catch a breeze under the only large tree in their yard, a wattle which had been overlooked when the block was cleared, and as he turned a page of his book, he saw a shadow on the ground. Tracing the cause, he quickly saw George, and gaped in surprise. He had not received so much as a line from Forster during the other's absence and, with other things on his mind, had not spared his friend a thought in months.

'Well, you can shake hands with me! I'm real.'

After the preliminaries, Kershaw led the way indoors to find liquid refreshment. Laurie was out visiting, the maid was enjoying time off, and he was alone in the house.

'I hope you remembered I was going to be godfather,' said George, accepting a glass, and quite unaware of how cruelly tactless he was. 'Went across to Bathurst to visit my sister before I came back here, and saw your family. They told me Mrs Kershaw had had a little girl.'

Then he saw the other's expression. 'Oh, Chris,' he apologised. 'Fearfully sorry. When did it happen?'

'Three weeks ago.'

Christopher did not wish to speak about it. Little Victoria, frail from the very first, had struggled on desperately until a few days past Christmas. She had been dead one morning when Laurie went to lift her from the crib.

For them both, it was more than grief at the loss of a child. The marriage between two people who were poles apart could be patched no longer. Her sister Estelle planned to visit Adelaide during February, and Laurie would accompany her. Christopher did not expect her to return.

'Your people'll be disappointed.'

'Yes. I'll be up to see them later this year. Now tell me about California.' As he spoke, Kershaw studied George more thoroughly.

George looked different. He was leaner, browner, and now wore a close-clipped beard, a decided novelty here in town.

They had returned to the shade under the tree, and George fanned himself.

'Forgotten how bloody hot it gets here in summer,' he complained. 'Never gets hot in San Francisco. Beautiful place. Only man is vile. Now, what's all this about you licking Steve Allard? Sydney was full of it. What was he doing here, anyway?'

'He and his brothers came down to see their sister. She'd had a baby, and they turned up for the christening.' Despite the depression and sorrow which hung so heavily about him, Christopher laughed. 'I'll never forget the look on his face!

It was worth living a lifetime to see.'

He was genuinely glad to see George. Forster was everything Laurie despised, vulgar, pushing, never too scrupulous when it came to making a pound, but he was also cheerful and sensible.

George downed some more ale, and stretched out his legs, before commencing the tale of his adventures.

He had known almost immediately that he had made a mistake. The trouble was, he liked his comfort. Ten years earlier, he would not have minded sleeping under the sky and taking his chance with the fleas and the cholera, but he was used to good living. Things soon looked desperate for himself and his nephew. Deserting sailors had left ships in the harbour to rot, and as there was thus no way of returning immediately to Australia, he had to do the best he could. With table tops being let out as beds for ten Yankee dollars a night, and Billie developing a cough in the foggy air, drastic measures were needed, so he got hold of a tent and set up a gambling place.

Chris could have no idea what fools some men are when they find themselves rich, he continued. Go right out of their heads. You'd see a cove who'd been slaving with a pick and shovel for months, fighting cholera and rattlesnakes and bears, spend a fortune in gold in two nights at the tables, and on booze and the wildest women a man could imagine. Not that the professional gambler's life was all roses. Some of the miners took their losses very seriously and George had Billie sitting up on a platform with a gun always at the ready.

Ironically, the greatest threat came from his fellow Australians. Drawn as if by a magnet to California, the worst criminals of New South Wales and Van Diemen's Land had formed themselves into a fearsome gang known, because of the canvas trousers they favoured, as the Sydney Ducks. They had their own squalid settlement at the foot of Telegraph Hill, from whence they raided and robbed and resorted to arson if their demands were not met.

'Fellow from Sydneyside of the Pacific called one day. Told me if I didn't pay him some of my takings he'd burn the place down round me. The Bird Stuffer, they called him. Never seen a worse type. Teeth like fence pickets and a neck made for hanging. That was enough for me. I wasn't going to pay tribute to any old hand, and neither was I going to be burnt alive. Heard there was a ship with about half a crew leaving for Sydney, and that was good enough.'

As he finished his story, George sighed, and played with the small piece of rough gold, a nugget he called it, which he now wore on his watch-chain as a souvenir of his Californian excursion.

'Funny thing, old man. Country up round Bathurst looks a lot like California. Pray to God that's as far as it goes. Gold's a curse, Chris. A bloody curse.'

Kershaw remarked that the only minerals ever found in Australia, as far as he knew, were coal up near Sydney and copper near Adelaide. Privately, he thought that some golden nuggets would be very useful indeed. His marriage may have been teetering towards final collapse, but his household expenses were still far too high.

A few days later, he knew that more than a few small nuggets similar to George's would be necessary to help him out of his crushing difficulties. As luck would have it, he encountered George outside the bank where they both did business, and, realising from the whiteness of the other's face that Kershaw was in a state of shock, Forster had taken matters in hand. Now the two men were seated in George's private parlour, where, not having had time to build up a defence, Christopher blurted out the story of his financial disaster.

His bank manager had that day received a letter from head office in Sydney indicating that unless Christopher Kershaw settled his debt immediately, foreclosure would follow. The reason was obvious. Stephen Allard was now on the board of directors, and this was his revenge for the incident on the day Prince's Bridge had been officially declared opened.

George fiddled with some papers on his desk. On top was a poster advertising the Anti-Transportation conference to be held in Melbourne within the next week. Back from California, the publican had lost no time in picking up his former interests. During his absence, the anti-transportation movement had been revived with the intention of ridding Van Diemen's Land of the penal settlement stigma which had been with it for nearly half a century.

'I'll tide you over,' he said, abruptly. 'I didn't enjoy California, Chris, but I came home a damned sight richer than I set out.'

'Oh, to hell with it. You might as well know, George. I'm finished here in more way than one. Laurie and I are splitting up. We've had our ups and downs, but with little Vicky dead, there's nothing left. We've been chalk and cheese all along. I'm getting out. Back to Bathurst, or even off to California.'

'Aren't you going to tell your wife? She might look at things differently if she realised what a spot you're in. You should try to patch things up. Both of you are upset over losing your child. Not looking at things sensibly.'

Christopher shook his head.

'Laurie didn't take it badly.'

He could not conceal his bitterness. He had wept unashamedly over the tiny body of their child. Laurie had turned away from the crib calm and tearless. 'It's God's will,' she had said.

George stared at him in that peculiarly impassive, flat-eyed way of his which had been such an asset during his brief career as a professional gambler.

'You know you only have to ask, Chris. And you should tell Mrs Kershaw. She has to know sooner or later.'

This Christopher knew he could not do. It was going to be hard enough to scrape up her fare to Adelaide, but after that, there had to be a regular allowance. He could never let the Fenwicks know just how deep was his failure. He was both a prisoner of his own pride and of his times. Women had to be shielded from the harsh facts of business life. It was their place to run the home and flutter about uselessly if they could afford it. Everyone knew that a woman's brain was not intended for the weightier matters of the world.

He did think briefly of turning to his father for help. From Joanna's regular letters, and from George's comments, he knew that Jonathon Kershaw, if not wealthy, was now very comfortable. But he had chosen to lead his life in his own way, and he would have to solve his problems in his own way.

He had resolved nothing when he called at Mr M'Kirk's chambers on that very hot Wednesday morning. M'Kirk received him civilly, and came straight to the point. Could Kershaw deliver some important papers to the owner of a store near the foot of Mount Macedon, about thirty miles out of town? It was an urgent errand, and M'Kirk had heard that Mr Kershaw had in the past performed such services for a fee. The young man was more than willing. He needed any extra money which could come his way, and, in the rough times ahead, every ounce of goodwill he could find.

'You'd have been within your rights to sue Stephen Allard for slander,' said M'Kirk as they parted. 'Still, I think you made your side of the argument quite clear to him.'

It would have been easier all round if I'd killed him, thought Kershaw, savagely, but at the same time, the idea of bringing suit against the all-powerful Stephen amused him.

At home to change into riding clothes, he went into the bedroom which he and Laurie still shared out of a mutual but unspoken desire to keep up appearances in front of friends and domestic help alike. She sat before a mirror, combing her hair, her expression disgusted. For no reason, every vestige of curl had disappeared, and as she pulled the comb through the pale blonde strands, her hair crackled and stood away from her head. There must be a thunderstorm on the way, thought her husband, though it is hard to believe with the sky so clear.

He was about to depart when, unexpectedly, she came after him, still wearing her loose wrapper, and her face pale and a little sweaty with the heat.

'Don't go, Kit!'

The intensity in her voice made him turn and stare at her.

'Why? Is there a dinner party I've forgotten?'

He had already informed her that he

would be away overnight, and that he had arranged with Hughie Deane to look in and see that everything was in order. His slightly sneering response was automatic, but even as he uttered it, he knew that he was being both unkind and ungracious. They were still in mourning for little Vicky, and there would be no dinner parties.

For a moment he saw the Laurie he loved reflected in her eyes, the warm, impulsive girl who had changed into this cold, moody woman.

'Never mind. It was nothing.'

That night, heat hung over the countryside like a weight, and Kershaw, trying to make himself comfortable on the tooshort bed offered him by the storekeeper to whom he had delivered the packet, thought he would never fall asleep. There was none of that lowering of temperature which came as a natural result of nightfall, and it was too far from the sea for the benefit of a coastal breeze. About midnight, a wind arose, a dusty, noisy wind, rattling through the gum trees, swishing dead leaves across the ground, and tearing strips of dry bark from the trunks.

This store, one of a cluster of buildings constituting a hamlet of sorts, existed mainly for the purpose of supplying the timber cutters who worked in the great forest which lapped about the base of mighty Mount Macedon, itself tree-covered to the full height of its three thousand-odd feet. The mountain had been named by an early explorer with a taste for Greek history, and some distance to the north, it was partnered by Mount Alexander. A bulwark standing out from the main Dividing Range, it was the most clearly discernible landmark in the fairly featureless Melbourne area, and when its purple hulk was particularly prominent, townspeople could expect rain.

Christopher awoke, very suddenly, again very early, just before dawn on that Thursday. He had been dreaming, one of those dreams so vivid that they shock one into wakefulness. He was suffering through a terror of early childhood, the day when a bushfire had all but engulfed the small cleared space in the forest which in those days had been the Kershaws' farm. In the midst of the flames and the fear, there grew a grass tree, in full flower. 'There,' said his father, 'I told you they only flowered after a fire.'

He sat bolt upright, sniffing the air, and in one reflex movement, was at the window, staring out, straining his eyes against the grey. Nothing. Still not satisfied, he pulled on his clothing, and went outside, staring about him and up at the overwhelming massif rearing to the dawn-streaked sky. A glow about half-way up to the summit turned into white smoke as sunlight hit the trees.

'Someone burning off rubbish,' said his host, stretching wearily as he came outside. 'There's always a fire up there somewhere. What a night. Hardly slept a wink.'

Kershaw could not feel as casual

about the timbermen burning off their rubbish in this weather as did the storekeeper, and he was eager to saddle up and be off. Still, it would have been impolite to refuse the breakfast prepared for him, and so it was past seven when he finally mounted his horse and set off along the narrow track through the forest. The sooner he was out on the open plains, he decided, the happier he would be, for the north wind was whipping up into a gale, bending the trees and cracking off branches, to the peril of passing travellers.

A flight of parrots screeching past made him look up, and for a split second he was cold with fright. The little white patch of smoke he had seen at dawn was now a vast brown cloud. Something fell against his hand. It was a small, charred piece of leaf.

He thought of the track winding ahead through some miles of forest, and then he recollected having noticed, the previous day, another path which crossed the main road, about half a mile further on. This, if followed to the west, should lead fairly quickly to open country.

His horse reared as two grey kangaroos bounded out from the scrub, hell-bent for safety, and for an instant the smoke cleared.

Oh, my God, thought the man, if I'm not out of here quick, I'll be fried alive.

The entire mountain, half a mile to his left, was going up in flames, like a volcano at the height of eruption. He reached his intersection, and conscious that he was trembling, drew rein to choose the safer trail.

Then, he saw them, about fifty yards to his left, on the continuation of the cross-track leading back towards Macedon. A man, a woman, and a light gig with a horse between the shafts. A tree had fallen across the way, and the man was frantically trying to shift its dead weight, while the woman, a screaming baby held under one arm, was attempting to grasp the flailing reins tossed about by the terrified horse.

An orange ball, feet across, floated down from the mountain-side, to alight, as softly as air, on the treetops not three hundred yards away. The branches which speared this balloon of flaming gas immediately crackled into fire, and the woman began screaming, too.

'Help us! For God's sake, help us!'

Kershaw examined this spectacle with a strange sense of detachment. There they were. Charles Ramsay, who had opened the crack which had turned into the rift between himself and Laurie, and his wife, Margaret, of the Allard clan, which had encompassed his financial ruin.

He barely heard Charles Ramsay's despairing cry above the roar of the fire storm, for he had turned his horse, and was on his way to safety along the westerly track.

A funny thing, but all this had started on a Thursday, too.

17

Laurie had awoken with a splitting headache after a night spent restlessly tossing and turning. She had thought to be glad to have the bedroom to herself, not having to lie tense on her side of the bed, conscious and yet afraid of his body only inches away. What had happened yesterday morning just as Kit was leaving? Something had come up from her inner being, a sensation so powerful that it had overwhelmed her. Hardly aware of having said it, she had begged him not to go.

It was the first feeling of any kind she had had in weeks. There had been a stirring in that icy little stone which had become her heart. She had wanted him to take her in his arms, but instead he had answered with chilling sarcasm.

This Thursday, the sixth day of February, was more than an ordinary

261

hot day. The air dried her lungs as she drew in breath, all metal inside the house was hot to the touch, and there was a tenseness in the atmosphere which was increased rather than dispersed by the north wind which tossed about the dust and filth on Melbourne's streets.

She sent away the laundress. It was pointless to try to iron clothes which were bone dry again as soon as sprinkled and rolled. And all the while, there was within Laurie this foreboding which no reason could erase.

The postman, parboiled in his uniform, was the one to impart the news which sent her running from the gate, a slight figure in a black cotton dress, her fair hair, still straight and dry, blowing into tendrils in the wind. At a high point where the intersecting street fell downhill, giving a clear view to the north, a small group of housewives, errand boys and the like, stood, silent and transfixed by the spectacle. Instead of Mount Macedon, purple and solid on the horizon, a column of smoke soared several thousand feet into the heavens. Laurie's hand pressed against her mouth. Distant clouds of smoke from bushfires were a commonplace of summer in Australia, but this was no small blaze racing through scrub until turned by a change in wind or the efforts of men. It was an inferno of a magnitude impossible to comprehend.

'There's fires everywhere', said a bystander, in that glumly satisfied tone which some people reserve for disaster. 'I was talking to a fisherman just in from the bay. He said that you could see fires in every direction round the bay just before dawn this morning.'

Even as he spoke, the black pillar wavered and dimmed as the sky above changed, in a matter of minutes, from hard pale blue to dusty brown, the bright sunlight fading into a sepia glow.

'Mrs Kershaw, is Chris at your house?'

It was George Forster, and surprisingly,

on this searing morning, he was dressed in his absolute best, dark frock coat open over a matching waistcoat to show off his heavy watch-chain and dangling golden nugget, and a beaver hat, held in a well-manicured hand embellished by a heavy signet ring.

'I went to the store,' continued George, in explanation, as she stared at him without a word. 'He's supposed to be coming along to meet the delegates to the Anti-Transportation conference. The ship from Launceston's been sighted, and we're part of the welcoming committee which is going to Coles' Wharf.'

He might have been talking double-Dutch for all she understood.

'He's at Mount Macedon. He's not back yet,' she answered, in a dazed manner.

'Where? What the hell's he doing there?'

'He had an errand. He's been away overnight.'

George digested this, and then took

her arm to escort her home.

'Now, don't worry, Mrs Kershaw. Chris has more sense than to wait round for a bushfire. Remind him about the conference, will you? Poor devil has so much on his mind these days he probably forgot.'

At the front gate, he added more reassuring words.

'If he left at dawn with his horse well rested, he's well on the way home by now. He'll be too late for the ship, so tell him to come straight on to the conference, will you?'

'Yes, I'll do that, Mr Forster.'

This was the first time Forster had seen Laurie since his return from California, and he was shocked at the change in her. There had never been any love lost between them, and their encounters in the past had always been marked by a careful politeness underlaid by a scratching dislike. He had always admitted that she was very pretty, but he preferred his women more down to earth. Now, the vivacity had gone, leaving her still pretty, but without life, like a doll.

There was something else too, which Christopher, too pre-occupied with the run of catastrophe threatening to overwhelm him, had not noticed. Laurie, always so careful about her appearance, had become slightly sluttish. There was a tear in the armhole seam of her dress, and even though it was black, it was noticeable to the fastidious George that the garment was not as clean as it should have been. There had been a time when, irritated by her slightly condescending manner towards him, he would have been glad to see her take a fall, but, on this hot Thursday morning, he felt an intense pity.

I'll bet, he thought, as he turned to leave, that the poor little wretch hasn't shed a single tear since that baby died. She can't. It's all knotted up inside of her.

By noon, Melbourne sweltered under a gloomy twilight, made more unbearable by the dirt-laden gale which swept along the streets, knocking over paling fences, whipping loose shingles from roofs and flattening the few garden plants which had survived the past weeks of drought.

Dust filtered in through every crack, and as the day wore on and the temperature reached one hundred and seventeen degrees, charred fragments began raining down on the terrified town.

No one had a clear idea of what was happening. Hughie Deane came to the house and told Laurie that there was talk of fires ringing Melbourne, but that, unless a blaze started right here in amidst the houses, the town should be safe because the paddocks on its northerly edge were mostly bare.

Late in the afternoon, there was a sudden change of wind, and cool breezes blew in from the sea, clearing the sky of its pall in an amazingly short time. With the sun shining in a normal way, and the temperature down a stimulating thirty degrees in as many minutes, people emerged from their homes to stare about them in bemusement. Ash and charred leaves lay in the streets, on every roof, and on every ledge and shelf. Before sundown, the day had already gained its historical title of Black Thursday. Burnt-out settlers coming into town from as near as Heidelberg, only a few miles upstream, brought in the first reports of destruction and miraculous escapes.

A steamer arriving from Geelong, forty miles away across Port Phillip Bay, bore tidings which horrified all who heard them. The little port had been surrounded on the landward sides by fearful conflagrations which had not only destroyed farms, cereal crops, animals and pastures, but had taken several human lives.

At sunset, Hughie Deane had given up all pretence of carrying out his normal duties, and stood waiting outside the Kershaws' front gate.

'I dunno what to do, Mrs Kershaw,' he said, time and again. 'I've bin to the *Argus* office, and I've bin to the police station, but no one knows much at all.'

'Mr Forster'll know what to do,' said Laurie, stirred into a sudden activity after a day of limp passivity, and without waiting any longer, she ran along the darkening streets to George Forster's hotel.

In the vestibule, she stopped, confused. There seemed to be a great many people there, most of them grubby and dishevelled, all seeking accommodation for the night.

'Mrs Kershaw!'

There stood before her a dirty, sooty, tangle-haired female scarecrow, recognisable, after the first shock, as Margaret Allard Ramsay. There was a blister in the middle of her forehead, and another on the back of the hand she extended towards Laurie. Behind her stood her husband, Charles, equally bizarre in appearance, with part of his hat brim charred away, and holding a squawling infant in his arms.

'Oh, Mrs Kershaw, has your husband returned yet? He saved us, you see. We were trapped, but somehow he freed our horse, and we escaped. I still don't know how. It was so — so dreadful.' The haughty young colonial aristocrat was now simply a young girl who had survived a hideous experience. 'We lost him. His horse bolted. Please tell us he's safe.'

Inside Laurie, the stone which was her heart splintered into a thousand pieces, and she fell into a dead faint.

★ ★ ★

George Forster wrung out another cloth in cold water and placed it on Laurie's forehead.

'Pardon language,' he remarked, 'but that Allard girl is as big a bloody fool as her mother. If not bigger.'

A waiter came into the parlour, bearing a tray with covered dishes thereon.

'Feel better if you eat something,'

continued George. 'You haven't, have you? Eaten anything?'

Laurie shook her head.

'It was too hot midday, and I didn't feel hungry this evening.'

'No wonder you're having the vapours. Sit yourself up, and eat, there's a good girl.'

Too tired to argue, she obeyed, and after a few minutes the waiter returned with a tea tray.

'A cup of tea, and you'll be a new person,' urged George. 'Now, I gather that Chris hasn't come back yet?'

Laurie shook her head again, and then sipped her tea, obediently. She was quite at the end of her resources, and content to let Forster, whom she actively disliked, take charge.

'No need to worry yet. Everything's confused. No one knows much at all. Chris knows most of the country round Melbourne like the back of his hand. He can't move much in the dark, y'know. Mrs Ramsay should've had more sense than to scare the wits out of you like that. They escaped. No reason why he didn't. Life's funny. If it'd been me, I'd have left 'em to cook.'

This time, she did react.

'What a terrible thing to say! Just because Kit and her brother had a fight! And I believe he's quite a horrid man, always partly drunk, and not really responsible for his actions.'

'It goes a little deeper than that, me dear.' George had sprawled into a chair, and his hard gambler's eyes watched her intently. 'Chris is broke. Stephen Allard used his influence with the bank to foreclose. He's finished.'

Laurie put the teacup down, very carefully.

'I don't believe a word of it! People don't do things like that just because they made fools of themselves when they were drunk.'

'Stephen Allard does. It's a long story.' He straightened up, and poured tea for himself. 'Point is, me dear, what are you going to do about it?'

Laurie shut her eyes tightly, and opened them again.

'I don't know,' she said. 'You see, Kit and I — we've agreed to disagree. It hasn't worked out at all.'

'So you're going back to your family, and leave the poor devil to sink on his own? Then why did you come running round here, eh?'

'Oh, be quiet!'

'I won't be quiet. Now listen to me, and stop acting like a spoiled brat.'

'How dare you!'

Laurie had had enough, and she arose, full of fury.

'If you're leaving, I'll see you home. You're going to listen to me, Mrs Kershaw. I can help your husband, if you can persuade him to swallow that pride of his. That's what landed him in this mess. His pride. He wouldn't let his father help him, and he had to let you think he was doing well when he was just managing from month to month.'

Laurie had paused at the door, and

now her knuckles were pressed against her mouth.

'Oh, no,' she said, helplessly. Then, in a much calmer tone she added, 'Walk home with me, George, and tell me what I can do.'

Outside, it was cool, with the stars shining in a sky so pure and clean that the events of the day seemed a thousand years away.

'Mrs Kershaw, I owe everything to Chris. Long time ago I played a dirty, low trick on him because I was desperate for money. I talked him into a prize fight, and it wasn't quite straight, and I did well out of it. He suspected what I'd done, and didn't talk to me for months. Talked my way out of it in the end. Ain't proud of it, but it was sink or swim for me. Been on my conscience for a long time. Like to help square things. What about seeing if you can talk him into accepting an interest-free loan to tide him over?'

Laurie laughed, a rather funny little

laugh with an edge to it.

'Aren't you forgetting something? Kit may be dead!'

They had reached her home, where Hughie Deane, sitting on a chair under the veranda roof, still kept vigil.

'Don't allow yourself to think such a thing. I'll be back at daybreak, and if Chris isn't here, Hughie and I'll ride out and see what we can find out.'

Laurie undressed and washed, and fell on to, rather than lay, on the bed. Her whole body called out for the oblivion of sleep, but her mind was too active for rest.

Why was life such a mess? She had always known how she wanted her life to be. As a child, she had wanted to grow up, marry a handsome young man, live in reasonable security, and raise a family of fine, healthy children.

This ambition should have been easily attainable. Her three sisters, even Louisa who had been so conceited and catty, had achieved it without too much bother. Instead, she had been pushed into a loveless marriage. No, that was not quite true. James had doted upon her, and she had been fond of him, even though he had been too old for her and had not fulfilled her romantic dreams.

When, by a miracle, she had met again the young man who had once filled her with such yearnings that she had embarked on silly secret trysts, it had seemed like a fairy tale come true. There could be nothing but complete happiness ahead with this dashing and passionate young man. Briefly, everything had indeed been like a dream, but then, reality, ugly and uncompromising, had interfered.

He worked irregular hours, he preferred vulgar colonial politics to musical salons, he had a temper, his friends were tradespeople, in particular George Forster, and she was bored.

As for the other part of the dream, the children, where were they? She believed she had not conceived during her first marriage because of her husband's failing health, for the seeds of his illness must have been growing within him even at the time of their wedding. She had almost given up hope when she had become pregnant with Vicky.

Once again, the reality was not like the dream. Instead of radiant motherhood, she had months of illness, ended by the premature birth of a child which she had known, from the first, could not survive.

How could she describe those few weeks of Vicky's pitifully short life? The little flashes of hope, followed all too soon by the instinctive knowledge that her child must die?

When she had realised that Vicky was dead, it was almost a relief. At least, she could go now through a day without expecting it to happen. Yet, it was all there inside of her, the terrible grief which could not escape, the anger against a world which had refused to live up to her expectations. She had been prepared to leave Kit for good, and return to her own family, where she could bury herself in their problems, in order to escape her own. It seemed an easy release from a situation with which she could not cope.

Now reality had slapped her across the face again. Her husband was missing, having vanished in circumstances of the greatest danger, and he was in serious financial trouble.

She put her hand out and touched his pillow, and then grabbed it to herself as she began to weep helplessly.

'Stop acting like a spoiled brat!' George Forster's harsh words echoed through her mind again and again.

Could that, after all, be the truth? Could it be that she was not the heroine of a drama in which fate continually played cruel tricks? Could it just be that she was a self-centred child who refused to grow up?

'God, please, please, send Kit back to me!' sobbed Laurie. 'I shall try to be a better wife to him. I shall, I shall.'

18

Whilst his wife wept into his pillow, Christopher slept at the side of a track about twenty miles north of Melbourne. He had stumbled to the spot just after dark, and worn out by this endless and frightful day, with a large burn on the lower portion of his right leg causing him near-agony with every step, he collapsed on to the earth.

As Margaret Ramsay had told Laurie, he had helped them to escape, although, as he would say later, it was more through luck than any skill of his own. He shuddered as he remembered how strongly he had been tempted to desert those hapless and inexperienced people, so foolishly trying to clear a path for their gig when sense dictated freeing the horse and running for their lives.

Thankfully, he remembered having noticed the previous day a burn-out patch a short distance along the main track. Half-stifled, they had managed to reach this place, about three acres in extent, where the terrain was sufficiently rocky and irregular to provide shelter from the waves of murderous heat pounding at them from the sea of flames all about. The gale which drove the fire at such speed, however, was also a benefit, for the worst passed by as the loose fuel was consumed. The trunks of living hardwood trees, even when bark, leaves and twigs are destroyed, are remarkably hard to set alight, and so it was that after two hours, the trio, with the baby grizzling and half-dehydrated in Margaret Ramsay's arms, decided to move.

With throats and lungs so dry that every breath was painful, they picked their way Melbournewards through the scorched and shattered woodland which now had truly earned its name of the Black Forest. Kershaw rode ahead, alert for danger and easier passage, and suddenly his horse, which had endured so much, quite lost its senses and bolted.

After some minutes of being carried through the smouldering trees and debris, he had been thrown, and had landed on a patch of cinders which seared his leg before he managed to jump upright.

For hours, his sense of direction confused by the near-twilight under the heavy pall of smoke, he stumbled through a blackened wilderness. He had never realised that so many creatures, furred, feathered or reptilian, dwelt in the forest, until he had seen their poor bodies, charred and distorted. In time, he came upon a small stream, where pools of water, surface covered with ashy scum, lay at intervals along a bed partly dried out by the summer. He flung himself into the shallow murkiness, feeling the bliss of moisture against his smarting skin. He drank endlessly, gulping down the muddy, gritty wetness as if it were a priceless elixir.

Now he had the chance to examine his leg. It was blistered, and extremely painful, but he had been saved from being burnt right into the muscle by the sacrifice of part of his riding boot. He found his pocket knife, and cut away the ruined leather to the level of his ankle to relieve pressure on flesh which was rapidly swelling about the burn. This done, there was nothing for it but to keep on hobbling, following the creek bed downstream. The wind swung round to the south, and the drop in temperature gave him heart to push onwards.

At twilight, he reached the Melbourne road, and walked towards the capital for about a mile before being so overcome by weariness that he fell to the ground at the verge, and slept. A shower of rain about midnight awakened him, and for a few minutes he saw a strange and eerie sight. On the slopes of Mount Macedon, and on the more distant ranges, innumerable small lights glowed, for all the world like those of a huge and spreading city. These were tree stumps which, kept alight by the updraught on the mountainside, had continued burning after the main fire had passed. The rain intensified, and he huddled miserably until it eased, but when he looked towards the mountain again, the lights had mostly vanished.

At dawn, he was picked up by a wagon on its way into Melbourne. The owner and his family had actually been camped not very far from where Kershaw had slept, and this wagon, the tired horse which drew it, and the clothes its occupants wore, were all that they had left in the world.

'I've a brother doing well over in New Zealand,' the man told Christopher. 'I'll never let my wife and family go through anything like this again. We're off to New Zealand to start again.'

'It's the sheep and cattle,' cried his wife. 'The poor beasts out in the paddocks! We could hear them screaming and bellowing. They were crying out for us to come and help them, and all we could do was drag our poor horse into the dam with us. Our cottage was burnt, and our barns, and only our wagon was left. I said, that's a sign from God. We're to go from this place and never return.'

Kershaw left them when they reached an inn some miles further along the road to Melbourne. He was ravenously hungry, but before he parted from this heartbroken family, he told them to call at his store when they reached town, and he would help them out with at least a change of clothing. What the hell, he thought, waving away their thanks. I'm ruined now. Let the Allards sort out the mess.

George and Hughie Deane arrived as he hobbled outside, George on horseback, and the older man driving a dogcart. No sight could have pleased him more, and George was able to explain why the Allards had been on that isolated track early on the morning of the sixth. Mrs Allard was suffering from a breast abscess, and on her way to Melbourne to consult a doctor. They had thought to save a few miles by cutting across country.

'She never once complained!' Kershaw exclaimed.

That was a woman for you. Carrying on over trifles, but able, when it came down to brass tacks, to show enough courage to put a dozen men to shame.

'And when we saw Mrs Kershaw early this morning she was ready to go to everyone she knows to beg clothes and linen. God, Chris, we've people coming into town from all directions, with almost nothing but the clothes they're wearing, and damned glad to be alive.'

For the first time, Kershaw began to understand that the fire at Mount Macedon had not been isolated. Melbourne had been completely ringed by fires, to a depth, it was now believed, of forty or fifty miles.

'Anyway, let's get you home. Mrs Kershaw's been half out of her head with worry.'

As George assisted him up on to the seat of the dogcart alongside Hughie Deane, a cart arrived in the yard of the inn, and a hush fell over the small assemblage there. The solemn expressions of the driver and his companion were enough to convey what the cart contained, without a glimpse of those blanket-wrapped forms.

'The policeman told us to come here. He's arranging for the coroner to be along. Family called Gilmore. Mister and Missus and four little ones.'

'Clara!' Kershaw and Forster stared at one another, and George ran across to the cart. After a consultation with the driver, he came back, his face greenish and shocked.

'They never had a chance. Oh, God in heaven, why do these things happen! They had a tall brush fence round their house. It caught alight and they were trapped.' George put out a hand to steady himself against the side of the dogcart. 'Excuse me, you start, Hughie. I'll catch you up. I — I want to ask about funeral arrangements. It's the least one can do for an old friend.'

Laurie was sitting down, hollow-eyed from lack of sleep and fatigue, when Hughie helped him into the house. Kershaw watched the emotions lighting up her expressive little face, the relief, the joy, and above all, the renewal of love, before holding out his arms to her.

'You were right,' he said. 'I shouldn't have gone.'

* * *

Some weeks had to elapse before a fairly complete picture of the Black Thursday disaster could evolve. The first impression that the fires had been confined to the central area about Port Phillip was soon set awry as letters and reports trickled in from settlers as far afield as Gippsland to the east, country north of the Dividing Range, the Western District, and as far west as Portland, near the South Australian border. This last had proved no barrier to the fires, for the tiny settlement of Mount Gambier in the neighbouring colony had escaped obliteration by minutes.

Reports ranged in content from tragic to slightly ludicrous, as in the case of the Portland residents who were most indignant at having their long-awaited race meeting ruined by fires sweeping down towards the harbour from the hinterland. The ship's master who brought this intelligence from Portland also reported his own alarm when cinders had alighted on his ship, then twenty miles out to sea.

Inquests followed one after another. 'Ran into flames.' 'Not seen again.' 'Died as a result of burns.' Matching these were the miraculous escapes, the party of theatricals trapped on the Sydney road north of the ranges, who lost their cartloads of possessions, but somehow survived; the bullock-driver on Mount Macedon, who, having freed his team as the flames bore down, grabbed one beast by the tail and was dragged to safety; the trapped shepherds and their sheep, who saved themselves and the animals by beating a path through the flames with green boughs — these were only a few. After a few days. Laurie Kershaw received a letter from her sister, Estelle, assuring her that she and her family were all well, that their homestead had been saved, but that their stocks losses were very high.

Superintendent Latrobe, with his new colony grievously stricken even before it had become officially Victoria, wrote to Sydney for help. Then, seeing so many settlers preparing to move elsewhere, he for once acted with initiative, and without permission from higher up, arranged for the issue of stores by merchants to those who needed them. In the meantime, some public-spirited citizens set up a committee to assist those most in need.

A few days after Black Thursday, it was noted with disapproval that

Melbourne's leading churchmen had not offered up prayers of thanks on Sunday that the town had been saved from the holocaust. The answer was crisp and realistic.

The inferno was of man's own making. Black Thursday was not a divine punishment handed down like the destruction of Sodom and Gomorrah. It had been caused by those innumerable persons who had taken advantage of the hot dry winds blowing down from Sturt's Desert, and had 'burned off' their stubble and unwanted scrub.

★ ★ ★

On Sunday afternoon, judging that her husband was now well rested after his ordeal, Laurie told him that she now knew about his financial troubles.

'George told me,' she explained, and then, reproachfully, she continued: 'Oh, Kit, didn't you think I was woman enough to stand by you?'

'Sit down here,' he invited, patting

the sofa alongside himself. He was sitting at his ease, his injured leg propped up on a footstool.

She obeyed, and he put an arm about her shoulders, drawing her against himself.

'And, Kit,' she murmured, 'do let Mr Forster help you. He wants to, so very much.'

'What a pair of plotters!' He laughed. 'As a matter of fact, I'd already made up my mind about that. Most of my pride burnt up on Thursday, Laurie, and that's the truth of it.'

Laurie, however, was not quite finished. There was something else very much on her mind.

'Kit,' she said, 'about the Gilmore baby.'

There had, after all, been one survivor of the Gilmore family, a minor miracle to come out of Black Thursday. When Clara Gilmore had been found, her body lay across a small pit, in which had been placed a four-month-old infant, the last-born of her steps-and-stairs brood. Poor Clara, with extraordinary presence of mind, driven by a mother's fierce instinct to save at least one of her young, had preserved the child's life by using her own body as a barrier.

'Of course. George told me yesterday morning. When we first heard about it, we thought they'd all died, but the little one had been left with the wife of one of the men who brought the bodies to the inn. Shocking business. Clara used to work for George as a barmaid years ago.'

There was no need to enlarge. Clara had died a heroine. Why sully her memory with squalid little details?

'Well, Kit, I heard this morning after church that Mr Forster is talking about adopting little Catherine. Oh, Kit, that would be quite impossible. Mr Forster has his good points, but he really isn't suitable.'

'She'd be better off with George than in an orphan asylum,' answered Christopher, not giving anything away.

'From what George could find out, there aren't any relatives on either side that anyone's ever heard about.'

She took his hand and pressed it against her cheek, and he felt moisture against his fingers as the tears sprung forth.

'Kit, I know she could never take the place of our little Vicky, but she's not much older and, well, I went round to Mr Forster's this morning after church, and she's the sweetest little soul. I picked her up, and she smiled at me. I know that we have to economise, but we do have a nursery already, and, oh . . . Kit, *please*!'

He never told Laurie that he and George had discussed the possibility on the previous day that little Catherine might become a member of the Kershaw family. The decision, he had assured George, had to come from Laurie herself.

19

On New Year's Eve, 1852, with 1853 only an hour away, Kershaw left the party briefly, going outside into the garden of the new house the Kershaws now occupied south of the Yarra Yarra. It was a still night, cool for summer, with the stars bright and heavy in the black sky, and he puffed contentedly on his cigar.

He certainly had not expected, as he battled his way through the sorrow and upheaval of 1851, that he could have reached this haven of financial security so soon. He often thought of what his father had said about the grass tree. It had to be burnt to flower. Well, he had been burnt, both figuratively and literally, and some personal good had come out of the Black Thursday catastrophe.

He could afford to smile now at the

letter he had received from Stephen Allard.

'My dear Kershaw,' the letter had run,

'I am writing on behalf of my brothers, and my father, Captain Allard, who, unhappily, as you may be aware, is now a complete invalid.

'My purpose is to extend to yourself our deep thanks for the assistance you rendered my sister Margaret and her husband, on the occasion of the disastrous fires on the sixth of February, this year.

'In particular, my father wishes to express his gratitude.

I remain,
Yours, etc.,
Stephen Allard.'

One could imagine Stephen gritting his teeth as he fulfilled the obligations of a gentleman, Kershaw had thought when he read this for the first time. He would have preferred that Stephen had ignored the episode. This swallowing of pride and writing a letter of thanks somehow still put the Allards ahead of him, and he was heartily glad that George had come to his rescue. Kershaw suspected that Stephen must have been very relieved when he found out that there was no need for a grand gesture over the foreclosure.

On the broader scene, efforts to re-establish the former prosperity of the Port Phillip District made little headway. Many settlers, who had lost everything and had been terrified out of their wits into the bargain, moved away, and by the time the first rains had brought up new green through the black, it seemed that Victoria would wither before it was officially proclaimed. The Sydney administration, distressed by the number of able-bodied men leaving for California, repealed the old legislation of convict days, forbidding mining for gold. Almost immediately, a Bathurst farmer who had gone to California, and had noticed the similarity between the terrain there and his familiar countryside, announced that he had found gold very near Christopher Kershaw's boyhood home.

'Mr Hargraves, eh?' Kershaw read about it in the newspaper when he returned to Melbourne after a visit to Adelaide with his wife and little Catherine. 'I remember him, Laurie. Well, just fancy, perhaps I should have stayed there!'

By April, the goldrush to Bathurst was on in earnest, and Melbourne business, which had been boosted by government funds backing supplies to those burnt out by the February disaster, fell away. Long faces became the order of the day as more people left, and even George Forster looked gloomy.

Christopher had almost made up his mind to move back to Bathurst — Laurie and the baby could stay with his parents while he tried his luck digging for gold — when he received news which almost broke his heart with vain regrets. His parents were both dead, killed in a driving accident.

The same mail contained a letter from George's sister, the one nearest the publican in age, who lived in the Bathurst district. After introducing herself, she announced that she was bringing Miss Joanna Kershaw to Melbourne. This was quite necessary, she wrote, as there were so many men of all types pouring into the area that a young girl needed the protection of her own family. She had, George's sister wrote, intended paying her brother a visit in the near future, so the matter would be one of mutual convenience.

It was not merely a matter of luck, as Kershaw soon found out. When the two men met the steamer from Sydney, Forster, instead of going forward first to embrace his sister, went immediately to Joanna, took her hands, and told her how distressed he was at these circumstances of their meeting again.

Joanna, ten years her brother's junior, nevertheless had a certain maturity of manner, and, Christopher soon discovered, a mind of her own. When they had parted from George and his sister, Kershaw immediately demanded to know by what right Mr Forster acted so familiarly towards her. Her reply was that she and George had been corresponding regularly, with her parents' blessing, since Forster had called on the Kershaws at Bathurst when he had returned from California.

'I hope you don't think I'll let him court you! He's too old for you, to start with.'

Christopher was furiously angry. George was his best friends, but he knew too much about Forster to want him as brother-in-law. Why, he spluttered, even that little nugget which George wore on his watch-chain had not been dug honestly out of the ground by George's effort. He had won it gambling.

'George told me about the nugget,' replied Joanna, a certain expression in her pansy-brown eyes. 'For myself, I like a man to have a bit of go in him.'

Laurie, quite against what her husband expected, thought that Joanna and George were well suited.

'I feel sure,' she said, 'that Mr Forster has quite repented of his wild youth.'

'Repented? George? Don't make me laugh. Only a few months ago, you told me that George shouldn't be allowed to adopt little Cathy. Now you think it's all right for him to be forever hanging about Joanna, filling her head with all sorts of rubbishy compliments.'

'Why shouldn't he? As far as they're concerned, they're engaged to be married.'

He did his best, but then something happened which set everyone in Melbourne, including Christopher and his women-folk, on their heels. Several businessmen, alarmed at the drift away of population, had offered a reward to the first discoverer of a gold deposit in Victoria. Traces were found within weeks, and at the separation celebrations on the fifteenth of July, when Latrobe was sworn in as governor, rumours were abuzz. The first finds were small, and with bitter conditions and snow on the hills, the first fever soon died away. However, late in August, when the bushland was aglow with golden wattle and the spring wildflowers were about to burst forth, the rich Ballarat goldfields were discovered.

The quiet, pastoral eighteenth-century days of simplicity were over. Kershaw now saw George's courtship of his sister in a different light. After all, he reasoned, George was eligible in the eyes of anyone who had not known him for years, and could not remember Millie Hooper, that prize fight about which he would forever have doubts, poor Clara, and the rest of it. Shrewd George was well-off, and not a fortune-hunter after Joanna's very nice little inheritance. If the Californian pattern was followed, and all manner of men began pouring into the country, Joanna could be best off under George's wing. Added to which, the couple were genuinely in love, the solid kind of love with mutual regard as well as passion. So, he gave his consent.

A few days before the wedding, brother and sister talked about their parents. The farm had been sold, and Kershaw's share of the sum realised would place him on a sound financial footing at last. Jo's money, at George's insistence, had been tied up so that she could receive the interest as a separate income.

'I'm glad they were taken together,' said Jo, as they sat in front of a roaring fire. 'They depended on one another so much, Kit.'

She had adopted her sister-in-law's habit of using the old-fashioned diminutive. She and Laurie had become good friends almost immediately, although Jo's calm, sensible and, as her brother had learnt, determined temperament seemed so different from Laurie's more mercurial nature.

'I'll always be sorry I didn't follow

Pa's advice and go into sheep. I'd have saved myself a ton of grief. Pa had his head screwed on when it came to money. D'you know, Jo, he must be the only small farmer I've ever met who did well out of it.'

Jo glanced at her brother sideways, the reflection of the flames from the open fireplace making her dark eyes reflect like a cat's.

'They're both dead, so it doesn't matter much now, with everyone off digging gold. Kit, do you remember the graves on the hill? How Pa used to gather up pretty pebbles to make them look nice? When I was little, I used to go to the creek when it was down in summer to help look for them. Only Pa used to find little pieces of gold. He made me swear on our Bible never to tell a soul, not even Mother. He'd an arrangement with Mr Aarons, down in Bathurst, and Mr Aarons would melt it down and make bangles and earrings and so forth, and go to Sydney once a year and sell them to sailors off ships.'

'But if he'd been caught he'd have been lagged,' exclaimed Kershaw. He was stunned. All these years, he had put down his father's increasing fortunes to solid hard work, and there it was! Pa had been quietly breaking the law by taking gold from the land and selling it.

'No one suspected Mr Aarons. He did some silver smithing and pewter work. And he'd been transported too, so he had to be careful not to be found out.'

'Well I'm damned!'

'Where was the harm in it? The creek was on our land, and it certainly made life much easier for all of us.'

This was logic, and the ultimate proceeds from that gold was making his own life easier. Jo's revelation had explained much, and made his vague suspicions of some years before, that his father had had a hold of some kind over Captain Allard, quite laughable.

He and George remained in Melbourne when everyone else, or

so it appeared, rushed off to the goldfields, and after the first months, as George had foretold, the immigrants began to arrive in their thousands, and the brothers-in-law found themselves making fortunes. Even with wages so high, and tradesmen so uppish, Kershaw's longed-for house out of the town was built, on a far larger scale than he could have ever expected two short years before.

It was little wonder that, on this New Year's Eve, under those same stars which had looked down on a filthy, injured and wretched young man who had stumbled out of the horrors of Black Thursday, Christopher Kershaw felt very pleased with life.

'Penny for 'em?'

George had come outside, carrying a bottle and two glasses.

'I was taking a breather.'

'Have some champers instead.' George stood carefully in the faint light from a window as he filled the glasses from the already opened bottle. 'Do you remember, old man, when we got horribly drunk on cheap brandy and hot water? I think it was your first night in Melbourne.'

They both laughed, but when George spoke again, it was in a graver tone.

'Forgot to tell you earlier. Heard today old Captain Allard died at last. Poor old fellow.'

'He must have been seventy-five,' commented the other.

'Not far off it,' agreed George.

'I only saw him the once. A fine-looking man he was then, though he couldn't have been young. That's when I pulled faces at the boys' caps, and lived to regret it. You wouldn't have thought anyone would have carried a grudge over something which happened when Stephen and I were about eleven years old.'

George had had a fair amount of champagne already, or perhaps he would not have mentioned it.

'Really believe that? More to it, old man!'

'What are you talking about?' demanded the other.

'Forget I said anything.'

'I'm not going to forget it. Damn it all, I nearly left the Ramsays to fry on Black Thursday. Listen to me, George. I saw them there, practically trapped, and I was so filled with hatred for the whole tribe that I nearly did something which would have haunted me for the rest of my life. If I hadn't tried to help them, it would have been equal to murder, George, so if you know why Stephen wanted my hide so badly, tell me. It was *my* hide, after all.'

George emptied his glass, and fiddled about with it for a few moments.

'All right,' he said, at length. 'Your parents are gone. The transportation system's gone. Our world's changed with the gold rush. It was like this. When I worked for Captain Allard, Old Flogger as the legal men on the place called him, he used to get really drunk every so often, and he liked me, so he'd call me in and tell me this long, sad story. He had a picture of a very pretty girl he used to show me. He nearly married her once, a long time ago. Only she wasn't in his class at all. She'd been transported, and she could hardly write her own name. He had to give her up when he decided to marry so he could have legal heirs. He picked on this widow, because she already had a little girl, and he knew she'd produce.'

'What has this to do with me?' Inside, Kershaw already knew, and something icy grasped at his heart.

'Don't get steamed up. You wanted to know. I'm telling you. The girl was your mother. She used to housekeep and all the rest of it, for Captain Allard. Old Flogger was very fond of her, bought her pretty dresses, had a flower garden made for her, anything her heart desired. But no wedding ring. Like me and Clara. Fond of Clara, poor girl, but it wouldn't have done in the long run. Always wanted to get on. Needed a wife like Jo, who can keep up.'

'Oh, my God,' said Kershaw, in a choking voice. 'That's my mother you're talking about.'

'Hear me out, old man. Old Flogger regretted it. I don't regret Clara. Sorry she died like she did, but I don't pine about her. Too fond of Jo. Wanted to marry dearest Jo right from the time we met when I came back from California. Old Flogger put his sweetheart out of his life when he married, but Mrs Allard used to keep on and on about it. If she'd kept her fool mouth shut, the thing'd have faded away. But Old Flogger had this little picture he'd had done of your mother, and he'd take it out of a secret drawer in his desk and show it to me. Practically weeping, he was, poor old devil. Swear I didn't connect it with your mother. She wasn't young even when I first met her, years ago.'

'She was near forty when Joanna was born,' admitted the other man. He was holding himself in tight control, otherwise he would have knocked

309

George down. 'And where does my father fit into this?'

'Coming to that. Never connected that picture with your mother, like I said, until I saw Jo again, all grown up and lovely. Jo's the image of the girl in the picture. Then it all fell into place, old man. Old Flogger told me his wife brought up the children to hate the woman their father preferred to her. She was crazy, of course.'

Kershaw allowed George to refill his glass. The wine was flat, and tasted sour.

'Your father, now, God rest his soul. He worked for Old Flogger when he was doing his time. The Captain liked him, thought he'd go straight from then on. Never mentioned names to me, old man. Well, he put to your father that he wanted someone to look after his Molly. He fixed it so that the man who took Molly off his hands would have a really good little land grant, not like the rubbish most transported men got in those days when they'd worked out their time.'

'But . . . ' Christopher could not manage another word. He knew that what George was telling him must be the truth. It fitted in so well. At last, he knew what was the favour his father had talked about. Jonathon Kershaw had married the woman who had been Captain Allard's mistress in return for being sure of a land grant good enough to support him and his family. Had there been an exchange of money as well?

His, Christopher Kershaw's, existence was due to a sordid bargain.

'However it began, it ended well, Chris,' said George, breaking into his friend's bitterly churning thoughts. 'I think poor old Captain Allard's last years must have been happier for knowing that his daughter's life was saved by his sweet Molly's son. Oh, come on, Chris. It's all history. It was part of the system. All gone now. We did our bit to see that it was gone for good, remember?'

George was right, of course. It had been part of the system, when it was not unusual for men seeking wives to go to the Female Factory and choose a likely-looking bride from the convict women employed there.

Then, perhaps because the champagne had made him lightheaded, he began seeing little pictures from the past. There was that afternoon in Christopher's childhood when his father had used precious time to make a flowerbed for his mother. Nothing could have been more wasteful when it was imperative to work from dawn to dusk for their very sustenance, and nothing could have made his mother, with her love of flowers, happier.

He could remember their alarm when they had seen Captain Allard in Bathurst that time when he was about eleven years old and had insulted the Allard boys. They had been afraid of having their happiness disturbed!

Jo had been right when she had said

that she was thankful that they had been taken together. Whatever their start together, for many years they had been a completely devoted couple.

Whatever else Captain Allard had done in his life, he had chosen wisely when he had asked Jonathon Kershaw to marry Molly. Could it just have been that Jonathon had had his eye on Allard's pretty mistress all along?

Suddenly, Christopher was glad that George had told him about his parents and Captain Allard, and for the first time he understood what his father had meant when he had spoken about the grass tree.

In the arrogance of early manhood, he had barely comprehended what his father was trying to say. Had Jonathon been referring only to the fresh start he had made in New South Wales? Could, rather, have the older Kershaw been talking of two people who had toiled and suffered together until, like the tall lily stalks of the grass tree after fire, love had emerged, raised itself, and bloomed triumphantly?

Christopher's own marriage had started in a whirlwind of romance and frantic passion, and when the madness had eased, what had there been? Two people who did not know one another, and who had come perilously close to parting before both had been shaken into the realisation that marriages do not grow without effort and goodwill from both sides.

Inside the brightly lit house, a clock struck twelve above the laughter and conversation.

'Before we go in,' said George, in a very slightly slurred voice, and holding aloft his half-empty glass, 'I'd like to propose a toast. To the Allards!'

'To the Allards? In the devil's name, why?'

'Why not, old man? If they hadn't made our lives so damned miserable that we had to escape from them, we'd still be honest sons of toil!'

Christopher Kershaw, jerked out of his mood of melancholy, roared with laughter, and slapped his brother-in-law on the back. Then, having drained their glasses, the two men went indoors to welcome what promised to be a very good New Year.

THE END

Other titles in the
Linford Romance Library:

A YOUNG MAN'S FANCY
Nancy Bell

Six people get together for reasons of their own, and the result is one of misunderstanding, suspicion and mounting tension.

THE WISDOM OF LOVE
Janey Blair

Barbie meets Louis and receives flattering proposals, but her reawakened affection for Jonah develops into an overwhelming passion.

MIRAGE IN THE MOONLIGHT
Mandy Brown

En route to an island to be secretary to a multi-millionaire, Heather's stubborn loyalty to her former flatmate plunges her into a grim hazard.

WITH SOMEBODY ELSE
Theresa Charles

Rosamond sets off for Cornwall with Hugo to meet his family, blissfully unaware of the shocks in store for her.

A SUMMER FOR STRANGERS
Claire Hamilton

Because she had lost her job, her flat and she had no money, Tabitha agreed to pose as Adam's future wife although she believed the scheme to be deceitful and cruel.

VILLA OF SINGING WATER
Angela Petron

The disquieting incidents that occurred at the Vatican and the Colosseum did not trouble Jan at first, but then they became increasingly unpleasant and alarming.

DOCTOR NAPIER'S NURSE
Pauline Ash

When cousins Midge and Derry are entered as probationer nurses on the same day but at different hospitals they agree to exchange identities.

A GIRL LIKE JULIE
Louise Ellis

Caroline absolutely adored Hugh Barrington, but then Julie Crane came into their lives. Julie was the kind of girl who attracts men without even trying.

COUNTRY DOCTOR
Paula Lindsay

When Evan Richmond bought a practice in a remote country village he did not realise that a casual encounter would lead to the loss of his heart.

ENCORE
Helga Moray

Craig and Janet realise that their true happiness lies with each other, but it is only under traumatic circumstances that they can be reunited.

NICOLETTE
Ivy Preston

When Grant Alston came back into her life, Nicolette was faced with a dilemma. Should she follow the path of duty or the path of love?

THE GOLDEN PUMA
Margaret Way

Catherine's time was spent looking after her father's Queensland farm. But what life was there without David, who wasn't interested in her?

HOSPITAL BY THE LAKE
Anne Durham

Nurse Marguerite Ingleby was always ready to become personally involved with her patients, to the despair of Brian Field, the Senior Surgical Registrar, who loved her.

VALLEY OF CONFLICT
David Farrell

Isolated in a hostel in the French Alps, Ann Russell sees her fiancé being seduced by a young girl. Then comes the avalanche that imperils their lives.

NURSE'S CHOICE
Peggy Gaddis

A proposal of marriage from the incredibly handsome and wealthy Reagan was enough to upset any girl — and Brooke Martin was no exception.

A DANGEROUS MAN
Anne Goring

Photographer Polly Burton was on safari in Mombasa when she met enigmatic Leon Hammond. But unpredictability was the name of the game where Leon was concerned.

PRECIOUS INHERITANCE
Joan Moules

Karen's new life working for an authoress took her from Sussex to a foreign airstrip and a kidnapping; to a real life adventure as gripping as any in the books she typed.

VISION OF LOVE
Grace Richmond

When Kathy takes over the rundown country kennels she finds Alec Stinton, a local vet, very helpful. But their friendship arouses bitter jealousy and a tragedy seems inevitable.

CRUSADING NURSE
Jane Converse

It was handsome Dr. Corbett who opened Nurse Susan Leighton's eyes and who set her off on a lonely crusade against some powerful enemies and a shattering struggle against the man she loved.

WILD ENCHANTMENT
Christina Green

Rowan's agreeable new boss had a dream of creating a famous perfume using her precious Silverstar, but Rowan's plans were very different.

DESERT ROMANCE
Irene Ord

Sally agrees to take her sister Pam's place as La Chartreuse the dancer, but she finds out there is more to it than dyeing her hair red and looking like her sister.

HEART OF ICE
Marie Sidney

How was January to know that not only would the warmth of the Swiss people thaw out her frozen heart, but that she too would play her part in helping someone to live again?

LUCKY IN LOVE
Margaret Wood

Companion-secretary to wealthy gambler Laura Duxford, who lived in Monaco, seemed to Melanie a fabulous job. Especially as Melanie had already lost her heart to Laura's son, Julian.

NURSE TO PRINCESS JASMINE
Lilian Woodward

Nick's surgeon brother, Tom, performs an operation on an Arabian princess, and she invites Tom, Nick and his fiancé to Omander, where a web of deceit and intrigue closes about them.

THE WAYWARD HEART
Eileen Barry

Disaster-prone Katherine's nickname was "Kate Calamity", but her boss went too far with an outrageous proposal, which because of her latest disaster, she could not refuse.

FOUR WEEKS IN WINTER
Jane Donnelly

Tessa wasn't looking forward to meeting Paul Mellor again — she had made a fool of herself over him once before. But was Orme Jared's solution to her problem likely to be the right one?

SURGERY BY THE SEA
Sheila Douglas

Medical student Meg hadn't really wanted to go and work with a G.P. on the Welsh coast although the job had its compensations. But Owen Roberts was certainly not one of them!

HEAVEN IS HIGH
Anne Hampson

The new heir to the Manor of Marbeck had been found. But it was rather unfortunate that when he arrived unexpectedly he found an uninvited guest, complete with stetson and high boots.

LOVE WILL COME
Sarah Devon

June Baker's boss was not really her idea of her ideal man, but when she went from third typist to boss's secretary overnight she began to change her mind.

ESCAPE TO ROMANCE
Kay Winchester

Oliver and Jean first met on Swale Island. They were both trying to begin their lives afresh, but neither had bargained for complications from the past.

CASTLE IN THE SUN
Cora Mayne

Emma's invalid sister, Kym, needed a warm climate, and Emma jumped at the chance of a job on a Mediterranean island. But Emma soon finds that intrigues and hazards lurk on the sunlit isle.

BEWARE OF LOVE
Kay Winchester

Carol Brampton resumes her nursing career when her family is killed in a car accident. With Dr. Patrick Farrell she begins to pick up the pieces of her life, but is bitterly hurt when insinuations are made about her to Patrick.

DARLING REBEL
Sarah Devon

When Jason Farradale's secretary met with an accident, her glamorous stand-in was quite unable to deal with one problem in particular.

THE PRICE OF PARADISE
Jane Arbor

It was a shock to Fern to meet her estranged husband on an island in the middle of the Indian Ocean, but to discover that her father had engineered it puzzled Fern. What did he hope to achieve?

DOCTOR IN PLASTER
Lisa Cooper

When Dr. Scott Sutcliffe is injured, Nurse Caroline Hurst has to cope with a very demanding private case. But when she realises her exasperating patient has stolen her heart, how can Caroline possibly stay?

A TOUCH OF HONEY
Lucy Gillen

Before she took the job as secretary to author Robert Dean, Cadie had heard how charming he was, but that wasn't her first impression at all.

ROMANTIC LEGACY
Cora Mayne

As kennelmaid to the Armstrongs, Ann Brown, had no idea that she would become the central figure in a web of mystery and intrigue.

THE RELENTLESS TIDE
Jill Murray

Steve Palmer shared Nurse Marie Blane's love of the sea and small boats. Marie's other passion was her step-brother. But when danger threatened who should she turn to — her step-brother or the man who stirred emotions in her heart?

ROMANCE IN NORWAY
Cora Mayne

Nancy Crawford hopes that her visit to Norway will help her to start life again. She certainly finds many surprises there, including unexpected happiness.

UNLOCK MY HEART
Honor Vincent

When Ruth Linton, a young widow with three children, inherits a house in the country, it seems to be the answer to her dreams. But Ruth's problems were only just beginning . . .

SWEET PROMISE
Janet Dailey

Erica had met Rafael in Mexico, where their relationship had been brief but dramatic. Now, over a year later in Texas, she had met him again — and he had the power to wreck her life.

SAFARI ENCOUNTER
Rosemary Carter

Jenny had to accept that she couldn't run her father's game park alone; so she let forceful Joshua Adams virtually take over. But Joshua took over her heart as well!

SHADOW DANCE
Margaret Way

When Carl Danning sent her to interview Richard Kauffman, Alix was far from pleased — but the assignment led her to help Richard repair the situation between him and his ex-wife.

WHITE HIBISCUS
Rosemary Pollock

"A boring English model with dubious morals," was how Count Paul Santana Demajo described Emma. But what about the Count's morals, and who is Marianne?

STARS THROUGH THE MIST
Betty Neels

Secretly in love with Gerard van Doordninck, Deborah should have been thrilled when he asked her to marry him. But he only wanted a wife for practical not romantic reasons.